USA TODAY bestselling author **Barb Han** lives in north Texas with her very own hero-worthy husband, three beautiful children, a spunky golden retriever/standard poodle mix and too many books in her to-read pile. In her downtime, she plays video games and spends much of her time on or around a basketball court. She loves interacting with readers and is grateful for their support. You can reach her at barbhan.com.

Endangered Heiress

BARB HAN

MILLS & BOON

First published in Great Britain 2018
by Mills & Boon, an imprint of HarperCollins*Publishers*
1 London Bridge Street, London, SE1 9GF

Large Print edition 2018

© 2018 Barb Han

ISBN: 978-0-263-07782-7

MIX
Paper from
responsible sources
FSC™ C007454

This book is produced from independently certified
FSC™ paper to ensure responsible forest management.
For more information visit www.harpercollins.co.uk/green.

Printed and bound in Great Britain
by CPI Group (UK) Ltd, Croydon, CR0 4YY

To work with an intelligent and amazing editor is a true gift to any writer's career. A huge thank you to Allison Lyons for being that gift to mine. I'm incredibly grateful for the chance to work with Jill Marsal, an amazingly talented agent.

I have so many writer friends to thank for friendship and encouragement. I'll start with a few: Elizabeth Heiter, Chris Keniston, Kellie Coates-Gilbert and Kathy Ivan. I love plotting books and getting #AllTheWords with you.

To my children, Brandon, Jacob and Tori, who are true lights in my life. I'm excited to see what adventures this year brings for each of you. And I fully intend to hit 1m before you, Jacob. Challenge accepted. Let the games begin.

And to John, who makes me laugh and keeps me grounded while encouraging me to reach for the stars. I can't wait to see what this year holds for us. I love you with all my heart.

Chapter One

Madelyn Kensington glanced at the screen of her phone as it vibrated. Her ringtone belted out. The screen read *Unknown Caller* and the number wasn't familiar. Everyone had gone to lunch on her floor and she suddenly felt vulnerable.

The area code revealed the call came from within Texas. Her muscles corded. She prayed this wasn't her ex trying to trick her into speaking to him by using a different phone. She had no plans to drop the harassment charges against him or ask the judge to lift the restraining order. She was still frustrated with herself

for allowing Owen to slip past her jerk-radar.
She'd walked away the instant he'd revealed
his true colors and, based on his threats, she'd
been too late.

A low sigh slipped out. This whole week
had been one problem after another, and being
without her convertible while the word *skank*
had been removed from her hood—courtesy
of Owen even though he'd denied it—ranked
right up there with the time she'd been stranded
for twenty-four hours with no bathroom during a road trip in college.

The ringing stopped and she stared at the
device. Tapping her foot, she waited for the
voice-mail icon to pop onto the screen. It was
taking too long. She absently fingered the small
dragonfly dangling from its chain around her
neck as she waited. The necklace had belonged
to her mother and touching it made her feel
connected, comforted when her life felt like
it was spiraling out of control. In times like

these Madelyn especially missed never having known her mother.

Owen's last words wound through her thoughts. *Think you can walk away from me? You'll never know when I'll strike.* Icy tendrils gripped her spine, shocking her with a cold chill that spread through her body. Either her ex was leaving the longest voice mail in recorded history or this was another frustrating telemarketing call.

Again, her ringtone belted out as the phone vibrated in her hand. The motion startled her. She dropped the device and pushed her chair back as her cell crashed against the tiled floor. *Great*—she probably just broke her phone over nothing. This needed to stop. She was jumping at every shadow ever since Owen's reaction to the breakup.

This probably didn't have anything to do with him anyway. Her father could be trying to reach her. She'd left three messages last week and another this morning to share the good news about her promotion as well as the special ceremony her old high school had planned for her.

Madelyn bent over and clasped her fingers around the phone. She hesitated. What were the chances her father was actually returning the call? It wasn't the first of the month. His calls came like clockwork.

Okay, she'd answer and then get rid of this jerk.

"Hello," she stated on a sharp sigh, deciding on balance that she needed to deal with whatever was on the other end of the line.

"I apologize for the interruption, Ms. Kensington, but I promise this call will be worth your time." The slight Southern drawl sounded educated and from Texas. "My name is Ed Staples."

"Okay-y-y." She drew out the *y* as she geared up for her response to the sales pitch that was surely about to come. The name Staples sounded vaguely familiar but she couldn't place him, so she spun around and typed his name into her laptop.

The man seemed to pick up on her frustration. "I'm the family attorney for the Butler estate."

She studied her laptop screen and, yes, received confirmation Ed Staples was telling the truth.

There was a pause and Madelyn felt like he was waiting for some kind of reaction from her.

"Are you familiar with Mike Butler?" Mr. Staples asked.

"Maverick Mike Butler?" she said out loud, not really meaning to. Now she really was confused. Of course she'd heard of Mike Butler, aka Maverick Mike. Her job at the *Houston Daily News* as an investigative reporter assured she would at least be acquainted with the name. His story was no secret—son of a poor crop farmer who beat the odds and made something of himself. He'd done so well that he was one of the wealthiest cattle ranchers in the Lone Star State. His rise to riches was as legendary as his buck-wild reputation. If rumors were true, he won his first ranch at a poker table and lost his first wife to his gambling problem. And that was where his run of bad luck had ended. Everything else the man touched seemed like it turned to gold. It was no secret that he lived on his own terms, another fact widely known to pretty much every Texan. Last week, the legend from Cattle Barge had made even bigger news with his death.

"Ma'am," the lawyer said.

The sound of his voice made her jump.

"Sorry—what did you say?" Outside of print, Madelyn had no idea who Mike Butler was. She'd never met him personally and they didn't exactly run in the same circles. "What did you need from me, Mr.—?"

"Staples, but please call me Ed."

Right. He'd already said that. Madelyn was distracted. Thinking about Owen had thrown her off.

"How can I help you, Ed?" she asked, refocusing.

"Can you meet me tomorrow afternoon here at the Butler ranch?" he asked.

"I'm afraid I'm working, but I might be able to arrange something if you tell me what this is about," she responded, still trying to shake the creepy chill from earlier. Owen was right about one thing: he seemed everywhere to her.

"I've been instructed to offer to send a car," he continued, unfazed by her work excuse.

"No, thanks. I have my own. Is there a reason we need to meet face-to-face? I mean, can you tell me what this is about over the phone?" she asked, mildly interested in what he had to say and at the very least thankful for the distraction.

"I apologize. My instructions are clear. If you want to know the nature of Mr. Butler's request you have to be on the property." He was steadfast. She'd give him that.

"Well, then I'm afraid I can't help you," she countered. Her frustration level was already high and she didn't need another person wasting her time. Plus, it wasn't like she could drop everything without a clear reason to give her boss and she didn't cover the crime beat.

"Would it make a difference if I told you that it's in your best interest to come?" he asked.

This guy was persistent. And frustrating with his cryptic message.

"Cattle Barge isn't exactly a few minutes down the road. If you want me to make that drive I need something to go on. My boss will want to know why I need time off to chase down a story outside of Houston," she said. When she really thought about it, the ranch must be swarming with media by now. Any news about Mike Butler's death guaranteed above-the-fold placement in print and major promo for broadcast. "Plus, there must be dozens of reporters at the gate chomping at the bit for something to report. Why tell me? I mean, just walk outside your front door and pick someone if you want to get your story out."

"This is personal," he said. "In fact, you may want to take vacation days."

Days? She decided to entertain him for just a second. "Okay, so let me see if I have this correctly. You want me to take off work at the snap of a finger for a man I've never met and a reason you refuse to tell me? Does that sound about right?"

"I'm afraid it's better than it sounds," he admitted.

"Who wants me there?" Maybe she could come at this from another angle to get an answer.

"Your presence was requested by Mr. Butler."

She waited for the rest of the sentence but Ed Staples would've made a great poker player.

"Pardon my directness, but he's...*gone*. It would be a little difficult for him to ask for me," she stated.

"I'm aware." He didn't give up anything with his tone. And she wouldn't even still be on the phone if he hadn't thrown out the name Mike Butler. But her mild curiosity wouldn't be enough for her boss to green-light an overnight trip. "This matter is urgent."

Hadn't she just read about his oldest daughter being targeted for murder? Was it possible the family wanted an objective reporter to confide in? Then again, that incident had happened after Butler's murder and the lawyer had said this was personal. If it was, wouldn't she at least know Mike Butler? And, again, why her? She exposed neglect in nursing homes and small business fraud.

"I'm afraid I can't help you. I can recommend—"

"Your refusal will come at a hefty cost to you, Ms. Kensington," he said firmly.

"No disrespect, but I have a good handle on what's important to me," Madelyn shot back.

"I didn't mean that as a threat." He sounded frustrated that he couldn't pick the right words to persuade her. A few beats of silence came across the line. And then, "Are you sure you want to walk away without knowing what a man like Mike Butler wanted you to be aware of? Out of everyone he could've picked, he chose you."

Well, when he put it like that she could admit the initial pull was becoming a stronger magnet. Walk away and she might never know what Mike Butler wanted to tell her before he died. Curiosity was growing the more she thought about it and a big exclusive could be huge for her career right now. She could prove to her boss that he'd made a good move in promoting her.

"Fine. I'll talk to my boss," she finally said, knowing full well she could get the time off.

"I'll email the details of your stay." The lawyer sounded pleased and a little bit relieved.

"I'll make my own arrangements." She'd learned a long time ago not to put herself in the hands of a source. And that was just how she'd treat this out-of-the-blue request, like any other news story she was covering.

"Be advised that you'll need to take off several days. I'd suggest a minimum of three," he said.

Wasn't that cryptic? She thanked him and ended the call, figuring she would take it one day at a time. Pretty much her new mantra, she thought.

For the rest of the workday, her thoughts kept circling back to Owen. Not even a hot cup of coffee could thaw the icy chill that crept into her bones when thinking about him. Nor could she shake the feeling of being watched as she walked to her vehicle after work—a feeling that was becoming a little too familiar. Madelyn had always been able to trust her instincts. Until recently. Until Owen. He'd knocked her off balance and she was still trying to regain her footing.

This, too, shall pass. The saying that had gotten her through so many sad or frightened nights as a child provided no comfort.

By six thirty the next morning, Madelyn had eaten breakfast, picked up her convertible from the shop and was on the road. She wanted to get out of Houston before traffic was too bad. The call still had her scratching her head and her imagination running wild. Dozens of scenarios had zinged through her mind when she should've been sleeping. But then, sleep had been as realistic as a unicorn sighting since Owen had made those threats. He'd been stalking her, too, and that had her scanning faces wherever she went, expecting him to pop up at the grocery store, gas station and every other place she visited.

Her thoughts returned to the call from Ed Staples. The lawyer had said this was personal but that wasn't exactly a new tactic to get a reporter's attention. It ensured she'd agree to the meeting without asking too many questions. Her mind ran around the same hamster wheel.

Even though she was a reporter, she didn't work the crime beat. Furthermore, she worked in Houston, not Cattle Barge, although Mike Butler's money seemed to reach all parts of Texas.

Did the lawyer want to leak information to her? Or was this truly personal as he'd suggested? She searched her thoughts and couldn't think of one logical reason she'd plan to stay on for a few days. What could be so important? Why her? Those and other questions that had kept her awake when she should've been sleeping had her yawning as she maneuvered onto the highway. Possibilities churned through her mind.

She tapped her fingers on her steering wheel, keeping time with the music on the radio. There was another good reason to get out of Houston. His name was Owen Lockwood. Dating him had been a mistake. He came from Houston oil money, family money, which she had promised herself she wouldn't hold against him when they first met. He'd been charming and polite on those first couple of dates. And then work had gotten even busier leading up to her promotion. Before she really processed their relationship, he was bringing her six-month anniversary flowers.

When he wanted to celebrate their milestone, all she could think about was how she'd lost six months of her life to nonstop work.

Owen had planned out an elaborate date and

said he wanted to talk about their future. *A future?* She'd almost laughed at him until she realized he was serious. Working fourteen-hour days, she barely had time to shower. The last thing she needed was the complication of a real relationship. And, face it, her time with Owen had been winding down anyway. He'd started to become possessive when they were out to dinner and another man smiled at her or looked her way.

When she'd asked why they needed to do more than enjoy each other's company, he'd blown up. His reaction seemed over-the-top. She'd told him as much. That was when everything started heading south.

Madelyn gripped the wheel tighter with her left hand and brought her right to her mother's dragonfly necklace. A migraine threatened and that reminded her even more of those last few weeks with her ex. He'd been the one to point out that she'd been getting them more and more frequently as their relationship had progressed. He'd insisted that she'd been spending too much time at work and insinuated she wanted to be with her coworker Aiden Creed. Owen had demanded that she spend all of her time off with him. And then he'd dropped the bomb that he'd been following her.

They'd fought. She'd told him it was over and he'd come unhinged. A man like Owen was used to getting what he wanted. He didn't take the breakup news well.

She'd filed a report when he broke her bedroom window. Another when he'd spray-painted the word *skank* across the hood of her new convertible. She'd saved an entire year for the down payment on her blue two-door sedan. Nothing had been handed to Madelyn and that was okay by her. She'd learned how to do things for herself at an early age.

It wasn't until she'd filed the police report against Owen last week that she found out about his past. The officer who'd taken the report looked her in the eye and asked if she was wasting his time. It turned out that similar charges had been filed and then dropped before anyone set foot in court.

Madelyn had been indignant and the implication that she'd cave under pressure fueled her determination even more. Owen wasn't getting away with his antics this time. She had every intention of standing up for herself and the other women who couldn't do it for themselves, for future women who would encounter the man.

Anger burned through her as she flexed her fingers around the wheel. Her grip intensified. When she really thought about it, spending a couple of days several hundred miles away sounded like enough time to let Owen cool off and get a grip. His bad deeds had been intensifying lately.

Besides, she really was curious about why

she'd be summoned to the home of Maverick Mike. Maybe he'd read one of her pieces and wanted to set the record straight about his personal life. Stranger things had happened.

Madelyn kept her eyes on the stretch of road in front of her, ignoring the tingles of excitement that always came with working on something big—and this had to be huge. Everything involving that man was immense. Traffic had slowed to a crawl and she couldn't see what was up ahead holding everyone up.

On this expanse of highway, she was beginning to see why everyone believed the whole state was nothing but oil derricks and tumbleweeds. The only oil derricks she'd ever seen in the city were on cocktail napkins. And, to be fair, she'd only seen a handful of tumbleweeds on the road so far. The closer she came to her destination the landscape began to change and she noticed there were more cows than she'd ever seen in one place. But then, Madelyn rarely left the city willingly. And she was going to a cattle ranch, she reminded herself. There'd be livestock.

Traffic had finally opened up on the 248-mile stretch southwest on a drive that had crawled out of Houston despite leaving early.

Her job had netted more than a few interesting assignments over the years but this request topped the list, literally coming out of left field. For one, she hadn't been working on a story that involved cattle, ranching or dead maverick billionaires. In fact, she'd had no association with the senior Butler although she might be one of the few women in Texas who hadn't, she thought as she rolled her eyes. What could she say? The man had a reputation.

Speaking of which, Butler's lawyer hadn't given her anything to work with, either. The man who'd identified himself as Ed Staples had kept the call short and sweet, promising her the message he needed to deliver would be worth the trip to Cattle Barge. Not even her editor, Harlan Jasper, could get answers. He'd made a few phone calls to see if he could dig anything up and had gotten zero. He'd thrown his hands in the air, pulled her off her current assignment, a piece on the real story behind the new districtwide alcohol-free campaign being implemented at local high schools, and had told her to make a story out of whatever information came out of the meeting. Even in death Maverick Mike Butler was news. Or maybe she should say *especially* in death. His demise had already created a media circus.

Leave it to a man with a big reputation to go out with fireworks, she thought. And even though her relationship with her own father was strained—well, that was probably a generous way to put it since she hadn't spoken to him in three weeks—she appreciated the fact that she knew what she was getting into with him. He lived in the same bungalow-style house she'd grown up in on the outskirts of Houston. He mowed the lawn at eight thirty every Sunday morning—no matter how many times the neighbors had begged him to push back the time even a half hour later. And he'd never remarried after losing her mother shortly after childbirth to negligent hospital practices, although he had dated the same woman for twenty-six years since. He was as reliable as fall football in Texas. And just to prove it, he still hadn't called her back. Her father phoned on the first day of every month, and any news—no matter how important to her—could wait until their monthly phone call, in his opinion.

Even though she desperately wanted to share her good news, her father didn't operate on the same excitement scale as her. There'd been more than work news. A few days before her promotion, her former high school swimming coach had called to say that she was being inducted into the school's hall of fame. Thanks to generous alumni donations, the school was getting a new wing. They wanted her to bring her family to the celebration. She'd almost choked on her mouthful of coffee. Even though she'd called her father right away, she was still waiting for a response. She seriously doubted he would change his schedule. He didn't like to upset his routine.

Madelyn wasn't sure why she felt compelled to ask him to go with her to the high school event. Maybe it was because he was getting older and she saw less and less time to repair their relationship. And she could never exactly pinpoint how it became broken in the first place. Her father loved her in his own way. She'd never doubted that. Her friend Aiden thought it was because Madelyn resembled her mother a little too much. She glanced into the rearview for a quick second. Did she remind him of what he'd lost?

Exiting the highway, she decided to table the

thought. She pulled into the parking lot of a small motel. She was roughly two towns over from Cattle Barge.

Madelyn desperately needed a place to cool off and regroup before the meeting with Ed Staples. It was hot. A drive that should've taken four hours had spread to a hard six and she still hadn't reached her final destination yet. She could already tell that the media circus surrounding the death of Maverick Mike had brought in news outlets from around the country. Traffic had thickened the closer she got to the small town.

Even though it was a very real possibility that Madelyn might be turning around and going right back home tonight, she'd learned a long time ago it was best to grab a room when she had the feeling a big story was about to break, and this one, two towns over, was the only one available.

All these reporters swarming couldn't be wrong.

Where there was smoke, there usually was fire. And she was curious just how big this blaze was going to get.

Chapter Two

The motel room was sparse but had everything Madelyn needed—clean sheets, a decent Wi-Fi connection and a soft bed. She set her overnight bag down, walked into the bathroom and splashed water on her face. There were eight missed calls on her cell with no indication of a return call from her father. She shouldn't be surprised but it was impossible not to be disappointed.

There were, however, repeated messages from her ex-boyfriend's lawyer. What was it all of a sudden with her and lawyers? As for Owen's attorney, no amount of calling or pleas would stop her. She had every intention of following through on the charges she'd filed. The next time she saw Owen Lockwood he'd better be explaining himself to a judge. And apologizing to her and every other woman he'd tried to manipulate and bully. She looked at her hands and realized that she'd been clenching her fists thinking about him.

Madelyn dried her face on the white hand towel before heading back outside and into gnarled traffic.

According to her GPS, she'd be arriving at her destination in thirty-seven minutes. A glance at the line of slow-moving vehicles in front of her said she needed a new system that could adjust arrival times based on traffic jams. In this mess she'd be lucky to get a quarter of a mile in half an hour.

To make matters worse, cars slowed down, stopped and then sped up with no clear reason. It went like this for forty-five minutes as she tapped her finger on the steering wheel. Her patience was wearing thin and especially since an oversize black pickup had been practically glued to her back bumper. She changed lanes. He whipped behind her. She shifted back and glanced in her rearview. There he was again. Was he afraid he was going to miss something? Because she could promise him there wasn't anything going on in front of them. Ten minutes later, they were still doing the same dance and the song was getting tired.

Madelyn pressed her brake, leaving a large gap between her and the car in front. The pickup wheeled around her, pumped his fist as he passed and then cut her off. She steered her blue two-door convertible into the right-hand lane to avoid a collision. Wasn't this turning out to be a red-letter day?

GPS said she still had twelve minutes before she reached her destination, which meant another twenty-five at a minimum. *Fantastic,* she thought sarcastically, looking at the four-lane highway. Before she could celebrate ditching the truck, a sedan came bearing down on her. Rather than tango with another frustrated driver, she put her blinker on to let him know she planned to get out of his way.

As she tried to change lanes, he whipped beside her. She turned to see what his problem was and caught the glint of metal. Shock gripped her. He had a gun. Pointed directly at her. Panic roared through her. Madelyn hit the brake. The white sedan mimicked her.

What on earth? The driver was going to shoot.

She slammed the wheel right and sped onto the shoulder. Horns blared and she didn't need to look in her rearview to know the sedan was following her. Gravel spewed from underneath her tires as she gunned the engine, her heart jackhammering against her ribs. Adrenaline kicked in and her hands shook. A gun being pointed at her had to be the equivalent of half a dozen shots of espresso.

Eyes focused on the patch of shoulder she navigated, she searched around for her cell with her right hand. She needed to call 9-1-1. The other driver was nuts.

At least this area of road was straight even though scores of angry drivers were going crazy on their horns. A truck popped in front of her, blocking her, and she had to slam on her brakes to avoid a collision. Her tires struggled for purchase on the concrete, spewing rocks.

The white sedan was closing in from behind. With the line of bumper-to-bumper cars to her left at almost a complete stop and the damn pickup in front of her, she had nowhere to go. Except right but that was a field. She spun the wheel, unsure of what to expect once she left concrete. Her vehicle wasn't exactly built for off-roading. Panic seized her lungs as she struggled to calm herself enough to take a couple of deep breaths.

She checked her rearview mirror. The sedan was tracking her. And she was running out of field.

HUDSON DALE WAS on his horse, Bullseye, when he noticed something he hadn't seen in the year since moving to the outskirts of his hometown of Cattle Barge—action.

A pale blue two-door convertible tore across his neighbor's land, kicking up all kinds of dust. Not far behind was a bigger sedan, white. Normally, he'd butt out of other people's business but this looked urgent, like trouble, and was headed his way. Besides, he could admit that his life felt a lot like watching paint dry lately. He was restless.

His experience in law enforcement had his instincts riled up as he watched the scene unfold. The convertible was being chased down and needed an out. As the vehicle passed by, he caught sight of the driver. He couldn't get a good look at her face, not with all that wheat-colored hair whipping around since her windows were open, but he could see that a female was at the wheel. She was getting bounced around pretty well in her small sedan.

Hudson strained to get a good look at the driver of the vehicle pursuing hers. He immediately pulled his shotgun from his saddlebag when he realized the male figure had a gun. Hudson loaded a shell.

"Come on, boy," Hudson said to Bullseye. He'd been named for the brown markings surrounding his left eye, making it look like the center of a target.

The convertible driver had nowhere to go and she seemed to realize it as she spun the wheel and hesitated, facing down the other driver.

Hudson whistled one of his loud, call-the-cows-home signals and motioned for her to head toward his gate. He aimed his shotgun, pumped once and fired a shot at the back tire of the white vehicle bearing down on her. Hudson's chest puffed out a little as he scored a direct hit. He'd been keeping up with target practice, maintaining sharp skills even though he'd never planned to need them again for work.

The convertible driver navigated wide as the other vehicle spun out.

Hudson managed to open the gate while seated on his horse. The pale blue two-door blazed inside the gate and he sealed off the entrance as he hopped off Bullseye, pausing only long enough to tie the horse off. His law-enforcement training had him putting plenty of mass between him and the drivers of both cars in the form of an oak tree.

Red brake lights stared at him from the back of the white sedan. The driver was making a choice.

"Put your hands where I can see them and get out of your vehicle," he shouted with authority, shotgun at the ready and trained on the white sedan.

The numbers on the buyer's tags were impossible to make out at this distance. The vehicle sped off. Hudson muttered a curse as he watched a suspect disappear. He angled toward the blue convertible that was still idling in his driveway.

"Hands where I can see them," he shouted with that same authority to the driver.

She complied.

"Can I move them to open the door so I can come out?" she asked, and there was something about her voice that sent an unwelcome sexual current rippling through him. Damn. It hadn't been that long since he'd had female company. Not really. Sure, it had been too long since he'd had interesting companionship. Everyone he'd dated since returning to Cattle Barge had left him bored and indifferent. What was so special about her?

"Yes," he said as he neared the vehicle.

The door to the driver's side opened and she kept her hands in full view. The woman who stepped out was stunning. Her wheat-colored hair fell around her shoulders in shiny waves. Her body was just as curvy, and, hell…sexy. She had long legs attached to what he could only guess was a sweet round bottom from this angle. Her full breasts rose and fell rapidly, no doubt from adrenaline and fear. She had cornflower blue eyes that were clear and bright. A couple of freckles dotted her nose on otherwise flawless skin. And speaking of skin, her jeans fit like a second layer and were tucked inside red roper boots.

Her hands were in the surrender position and she didn't bother to close her vehicle's door. Good moves. He also noticed that there wasn't a gold band on her ring finger. Didn't always mean someone wasn't married, but was a pretty good indicator. He lied to himself when he said the only reason he'd noticed was habit.

"What the hell was that?" he asked, ignoring his other thoughts—thoughts that had no business creeping in while he investigated a possible crime. Speaking of which, this whole scene had *angry boyfriend* written all over it.

"Thank you for helping me," she said and her voice shook. She also had an almost imperceptible drawl. She was from Texas. "I have no idea what's going on. This guy came out of nowhere aiming a gun at me."

She looked completely rattled. Her eyes— eyes that were almost a perfect match to her convertible—were wild, and she had that desperate look he'd seen one too many times on victims and especially on Misty when…

Hudson refused to go over that again. Not even in his mind.

He could clearly see that this woman's hands

shook. And her eyes had that bewildered quality that victims often had when they didn't see a crime coming.

Hudson believed her. "Do you have a weapon?"

"No." She glanced around and his gaze dropped to her jean pockets for confirmation. A serious mistake in his opinion because stray voltage zapped him and a thunderclap of need followed, sizzling through him.

"Where are you headed?" He blew out a sharp breath. Those emotions had no business in this conversation. He'd call the sheriff, turn her over and get back to his day.

"I'm Madelyn Kensington, by the way," she said, offering a handshake.

He took it, and did his level best not to notice the fact that her skin was as silky as it looked. "Hudson Dale."

"What branch of law enforcement do you work in?" she asked, dropping her hands to her sides. He didn't mind the move. There was no way she was carrying a weapon anywhere in those jeans.

Her question caught him off guard. "What makes you think I'm anything more than a rancher?"

She glanced at his legs. "Your posture. The way you hold that shotgun. You walk with your arms out a little, like you're still wearing a holster, and your aim with that shotgun is pretty dead accurate."

He put a hand up to stop her. "I'm no such thing. What kind of work do you do that makes you notice the way a man carries himself?"

"Me? I'm a reporter from Houston headed to the Butlers," she said, and he was close enough to see her erratic heartbeat pound at the base of her neck.

The last thing Hudson needed was someone who knew how to do research nosing around in his business and especially his past. And there'd been plenty of journalists in the area following the death of Maverick Mike.

"Well, right now, Mrs. Kensington—"

"It's Miss," she corrected.

He gave a curt nod of acknowledgment even though an inappropriate reaction stirred in his chest.

"Is there any chance that white sedan belongs to your boyfriend?" he asked.

"I don't have one, but I do have a persistent ex," she admitted.

Why did relief wash over him when he heard those words? He'd noticed her ring finger a minute ago and tried not to care one way or the other when he didn't see a gold band.

"The guy who just ran you off the road is getting away." Hudson fished his cell out of his back pocket, keeping an eye on the reporter. "So, if you don't mind, I need to make a call to the sheriff's office and see if we can stop him before someone else gets hurt."

"Yes, by all means," she said, taking a step back and leaning a hip against the side of her trunk. She folded her arms and he noticed how the move pushed her breasts against the spring-green cotton shirt she wore. Calmer, her voice was as creamy and smooth as her skin.

Hudson forced his gaze away from the wheat-haired beauty. Getting involved with a woman like her was dangerous. Emotions had no place in an investigation. And he had no intention of repeating past mistakes.

Chapter Three

Madelyn's pulse hammered her ribs. Hudson Dale might look like a cowboy in those low-slung jeans, dark navy T-shirt with rolled-up sleeves and white Stetson, but something—call it reporter instincts and keen observation skills—told Madelyn that he was hiding something. Would that something put her in more danger?

The man had that law-enforcement swagger when he walked but hadn't identified himself as such. He even sounded law enforcement when he'd instructed her to get out of the car with that commanding voice of his—a voice that traveled over her with an inappropriate sensual shiver that ran down her back.

When she'd outright asked, he denied ever working the job. She'd spent enough time around cops when she worked the crime beat early on in her career to recognize the voice of authority they used when they spoke to someone. This guy looked far too young to be retired. The man couldn't be a day older than thirty-two, which was only two years older than Madelyn.

He was either undercover, or…

He could've been fired. Hiding. Why else would he move to the outskirts of a small town? Then again, maybe he just wanted peace and quiet.

Madelyn tried not to let her imagination run away with her. Either way, she was grateful that he'd been there to help when she needed it. Noticing the fact that the man was gorgeous couldn't be helped. He was standing right in front of her. They were barely five feet apart, so it was easy to take note that he had the darkest brown eyes she'd ever seen highlighted by sandy-blond hair and a dimpled chin. Her nerves were heightened and that was why her body was having an out-of-place reaction. She also tried to convince herself that the only reason she considered his rippled chest and muscled arms was basic survival instinct. On a primal level she needed to know that this man was strong enough to defend her should the white sedan come back for another round. The fact that he seemed more than capable kept her nerves a couple of notches below panic.

"The sheriff is on his way and you look like you could use a cup of coffee." Hudson motioned toward the ranch-style house. "Since I'm not sure it's a good idea to leave you alone on my property, you'd better come inside with me."

She nodded. The man was unnervingly cool

considering he'd just had to shoot out someone's tire to get them to leave his land.

"Your car should be fine where it is," he said, his horse still tied up near the gate in the shade.

"Thank you." She followed the handsome cowboy inside his house. The decor looked comfortable, simple. A couch and matching love seat surrounded a tumbled stone fireplace with a large rustic star over the mantel. There was a bronze statue of a bull rider on the sofa table and twin lamps that looked good for reading light.

The kitchen was simple—white cabinets, stainless-steel appliances and marbled granite. She leaned against the bullnose edging, trying to absorb everything that had just happened.

"Care to fill me in on what's going on?" Hudson asked, offering her a fresh cup of coffee.

Madelyn took the mug and gripped it with both hands, noticing that she was still shaking. She chalked it up to adrenaline. Owen had nearly run her off the road recently, trying to get her attention. He'd seemed more desperate to speak to her than deadly at the time. But he drove an Escalade, not a white sedan. Of course, logic said he could've rented one.

"I had a bad breakup and he might be following me." She had to consider that possibility, especially since she hadn't gotten a good look at the driver. Of course, with Owen's money he could've hired someone to scare her.

The cowboy's jaw muscle clenched and released. He blinked the thickest lashes. "Is the law aware?"

"A judge in Houston issued a restraining order." She reached for her necklace and found comfort in holding her mother's dragonfly. "I couldn't get a good enough look at the driver to know if that was him. That's not his car."

"Is he dumb enough to drive his own if he pulled a stunt like this?" Hudson asked.

"No." Owen wasn't stupid. "He has a lot of money. Enough to hire someone to be discreet."

"Does he have a record?" Hudson's eyebrow arched.

"Yes," she hated to admit. She sipped the fresh coffee, welcoming the burn on her tongue. "I didn't find out about it until it was too late. I'm sure that he was only trying to scare me before. This is something totally different. I hope it's not him."

The cowboy's steady gaze seemed locked onto an idea.

"What are you thinking?" she asked, realizing that she was gripping her mug so tight that her knuckles were sheet-white.

"That it's him and he's escalating," he said, shooting her a look.

"He's a jerk, I'll give you that, but he's not... I mean, *that guy* seemed like he was trying to kill me. Owen threatened me but he was trying to intimidate me to get back together with him. I wouldn't be able to do that dead."

The cowboy didn't respond and the quiet rang in her ears.

And then it dawned on her that he was probably thinking Owen had decided that if he couldn't have her no one would.

The doorbell rang before she could rationalize that idea. The cowboy set down his mug before picking up his shotgun. He loaded a slug in the shotgun's chamber and readied it on his shoulder. "Whoever it is won't get to you on my watch."

Madelyn was momentarily too shocked to move as another shot of adrenaline coursed through her. Her heartbeat drummed in her ears. Could Owen hate her that much? Could he be that selfish? Yes, he'd crossed a few lines and had gotten away with it until now. But would he go so far as to want her dead? She'd covered stories that still made her shudder to think about them in the same context as her relationship with Owen.

The sheriff walked in and introduced himself as Clarence Sawmill. He was middle-aged, and his eyes had the white outline of sunglasses on otherwise tanned skin. Deep grooves in his forehead, hard brackets around his mouth and his tight grip on a coffee mug outlined the man's stress level. He was on high alert and, from the looks of him, had been since news broke of Maverick Mike's murder.

"Wish we were meeting under better circumstances, Sheriff Sawmill," Madelyn conceded, taking the hand being offered in a vigorous shake.

"I'd like to hear what happened," he said with a polite nod. The sheriff was considerably shorter than the cowboy, who had to be at least six foot three, and he wasn't nearly as in shape. Sawmill squared his shoulders. His forehead creased with concern as Madelyn recalled the events, horrified at the thought Owen could be behind the attack. She wouldn't deny the possibility. And she tried not to notice how intent the cowboy seemed at picking up every last detail of her statement. One look at him said he had to have been on the job. And it might not be her business but she wanted to know more about the quiet cowboy.

Sawmill listened. "Did the driver fire at you?"

"No, he didn't."

"We've had a few similar incidents on the highway lately. Cases of road rage have doubled with the August sun and the town is still in a frenzy over the death of one of our residents." Sawmill's shoulders seemed in a permanent slump and his posture gave away his weariness. No doubt this was the first time he'd dealt with a high-profile murder on what he'd see as "his watch." The intensity of his expression said he cared about doing a good job.

Road rage? She prayed it was that simple because the other was unthinkable.

"Is there a number where I can reach you if I have more questions?" Sawmill asked.

Madelyn relayed her cell number. "I'm staying at the Red Rope Inn for a couple of days if you need to find me."

The sheriff nodded. "I'll make a note on your file."

"Thank you for your time," Madelyn said as she followed him out the door. She scanned the horizon as a cold prickly feeling came over her, like eyes watching her. But there was no one around.

Before the sheriff disappeared she'd handed her empty mug to the cowboy. "Thanks for your help. I'm not sure what I would've done if you hadn't been there."

He tipped his hat but didn't respond as he followed her onto the lawn. "Keep watch in case he returns."

"You think he'll come back?" Her heart drummed her rib cage.

"Probably not. He'll have to fix his tire and regroup," he said. "Doesn't hurt to be extra careful."

Madelyn thanked the cowboy again before sliding into the driver's seat. Her palms were sweaty and her heart still galloped but she'd been threatened in her job before. It would take more than a stressful brush with road rage—if the sheriff had accurately assessed the situation—to detour her from finding out what Maverick Mike wanted with her.

Now that she'd almost made it to the ranch, her curiosity was at an all-time high. And she couldn't think of one reason the man would summon her.

THERE HAD TO be two dozen news trucks lining the street in front of the Hereford Ranch due to Maverick Mike's murder. Again, Madelyn questioned what she was doing here. If there was a story, wouldn't one of these reporters have already sniffed it out?

A beefy security guy stood at the gate attached to a white log fence. He was wearing navy shorts and a matching button-down short-sleeved shirt, and had a gun strapped to his hip.

She rolled her window down and gave her name along with the name of the paper where she worked.

Beefy's dark brow arched.

"I'm expected," she added to clarify.

"Name again, please," he said, checking his tablet.

"Madelyn Kensington." She couldn't get a good look at his eyes through his mirrored sunglasses. The guy obviously worked out but he had nothing on the cowboy from earlier.

Beefy tilted his head to the side. "Main building is straight ahead. Go on through."

"Thank you," she said, pulling away and

kicking up a lot of dirt as she navigated into a parking spot near the main building's entrance. She grabbed her purse and stepped out of her car, dusting off her jeans, thinking how much she loved living in the city. The ranch was beautiful, don't get her wrong, but checking her boots for scorpions before she put them on wasn't exactly her idea of fun.

The main building looked like an oversize log cabin. It had more of a Western high-end resort feel with rustic accents. She slipped her purse strap over her shoulder and walked toward the door. Before she could reach for the knob, the door swung open. She had to put a hand up to stop it from smacking her in the face.

"My apologies," the man wearing a taupe business suit with cowboy boots topped off by a cream-colored Stetson said with a smile of appreciation. "We spoke on the phone earlier. I'm Ed."

Madelyn introduced herself as she took his

outstretched hand. His shake was firm and quick, his expression concerned.

"Sorry I'm late. I had a difficult time getting here today," she confided.

"Do you mind filling me in on that?" he asked with a raised brow.

"I've already given my report to the sheriff." And then it dawned on her why he'd ask. Ella Butler had just survived an attempted murder. Madelyn shook her head. "No, it's nothing. Sheriff thinks it's a case of road rage." She didn't want to get into the fact that it could've been Owen with a stranger.

"I see. You're no doubt aware of the situation the Butler family is dealing with," he said with a sympathetic look, and she couldn't help but notice that he was scanning her face. But for what? He seemed to be intensely staring at the bridge of her nose and it was making her a little self-conscious. Her nose had always had a slight bump and she'd sworn that she would get a nose job someday as a teenager.

Ed nodded and his lip curled into a faint grin. He was looking at her like she was some piece of artwork to be examined, like he was searching for something.

"Yes. I'm sorry for the loss of their father and for the criminal activity surrounding it," she said honestly. She didn't know the family, but a quick Google search last night had revealed a snapshot of what they'd been going through. No one deserved this kind of attention. She was getting irritated at the way he was staring at her. "Forgive my confusion, but what is so urgent that you needed to see me right away?"

He seemed to catch on when she used her you're-being-rude tone.

"I apologize for my behavior." He shook his head and made a production of walking in the opposite direction toward an office with glass-

and-wooden French doors. "I'd prefer to have this conversation in private."

Madelyn glanced around, didn't see another soul. The place was beautiful, though. So far she'd endured a crazy driver, a cowboy who rattled her with his calm demeanor, and now she was with a lawyer who needed to get to the point. She had no idea what was going on with people today, but she'd hit her limit and was starting to get annoyed.

She stalked behind the lawyer into the office. Floor-to-ceiling bookshelves covered the walls. She was almost distracted by the rare book collection when she decided it was more important to know the real reason she was standing in what had to be Maverick Mike Butler's private study. If it wasn't for the day she'd been having, she might actually enjoy all of this. Seriously, this guy was legend and how many times in her life would she actually get to stand in the study of such a notorious, successful and eccentric man?

The problem was that her nerves were still fried from the drive over and her thoughts kept wandering to the handsome cowboy who'd literally ridden up on his horse and saved her. Call it Old West nostalgia, but he did make her pulse race just thinking about him. That was the thing about living in Texas. Anything could happen.

Ed put on glasses and took a seat in the executive chair. He motioned toward a leather club chair opposite the massive desk. She took a seat, crossed her legs and placed her folded hands in her lap, figuring this day couldn't possibly get any worse.

He mumbled another apology before locating an envelope and making an "ah-ha" sound. He pushed black-rimmed spectacles up the bridge of his nose.

Madelyn realized she'd lifted her hand to her

mother's necklace as she fingered the details of the dragonfly.

"Forgive me for saying, but…" He paused and then seemed to think otherwise as he stared at the envelope.

She caught his stare and a feeling rippled through her. She couldn't exactly pinpoint what it was but that look in his eyes sent a shiver racing down her spine, like the kind when people said a cat walked over a grave.

Ignoring the prickly-pin feeling on her arms, she half expected him to get up and walk out of the room when he tossed the envelope in her direction. Many a news lead was "handed" over in similar fashion.

Instead of excusing himself, he leaned back in his chair and continued examining her.

"What's in that envelope is yours to keep. I've been instructed by the late Mr. Butler to advise you to think heavily on it before you break that seal. There'll be no going back once you know what that envelope contains and the information will change your life forever." She listened for something in Ed Staples's tone to indicate that this was some kind of joke. The intensity of his stare said that it wasn't. And now her curiosity really was hitting full peak.

"I doubt that, Mr. Staples." She picked up the white envelope.

"Don't be so sure," he said. "You should take a moment to consider whether or not you're ready."

She ripped open the flap in one swipe and pulled out the 8-1/2 by 11 sheet of paper. It was trifold, so she flatted out the page. "All I'm ready for is a hot bath, a glass of wine and a…"

Madelyn froze. A gasp escaped.

There was no way. This had to be some kind of twisted joke. She glanced up, looking for cameras. Was she on one of those prank shows?

"I can assure you this is legitimate," Ed said,

but his voice disappeared in the background noise exploding in her head.

She would know something like this. Some-one would've said something to her before now.

"I know who my father is and it isn't Mike Butler." The words were barely audible even to her as she pulled out the legal document that declared her his legal child. Madelyn cleared her throat. "There's been a mistake."

And then Ed Staples said the words she least wanted to hear. "I'm afraid not. It's true."

Madelyn gripped the piece of paper. The edges crinkled in her hand.

"I've never even met this man. This can't be—"

Ed sat there, looking like he had a well of patience to draw on. And then he said, "Who do you think gave your mother that necklace you're wearing?"

Those words exploded in her head. She was on her feet fast and racing toward the door before she could even begin to process. The day her father had given her the trinket popped into her thoughts. He'd looked so grieved when she opened the gift on her fifteenth birthday. Her mother had given him death-bed instructions to make sure Madelyn received it. He'd looked so pained as she opened the box. Until now, Madelyn had always believed that the necklace reminded him of her mother. Could his expression have meant something else? Was it a reminder of the affair she'd had?

Madelyn didn't bother to look back to see if Ed Staples had followed her. All she needed was a quiet room and a way to rewind this crazy day.

With every step toward her pale blue convertible, a little more life escaped from her. A shot of adrenaline was the only thing keeping her legs moving, her flee response having kicked into high gear. Her chest squeezed and it felt like her lungs were seizing.

Hands shaking, she took a few tries to get the letter unstuck from the moisture gathered on her fingers and grip her car key.

She wasn't sure how she managed to get the key in the ignition and start her car. It was all a blur. Was her entire life a lie? A secret this big couldn't be hidden for thirty years...*could it*?

Tears blurred her vision. She blinked them away the best she could and focused on getting the hell out of there. Time seemed to slow as Madelyn tried to process the possibility of Mike Butler being her birth father. Maverick Mike Butler.

One hand on the wheel, she absently fingered the delicate silver dragonfly dangling from its chain as the log-style home shrank in the rearview mirror.

Madelyn parked in front of her motel room. Her limbs felt like hundred-pound weights and her body sank deeper into the driver's seat. She managed to pick up her phone and dial her father's number.

Of course, he didn't pick up. *Why would he start now*, she thought bitterly.

Madelyn forced herself out of her car and into her motel room. The second she walked in, something felt off. Hadn't she placed her laptop on the second bed, not the one closest to the door? Her overnight bag was unzipped and some of the contents spilled out. On the mirror at the back of the wall were scribbled large letters in what looked like red lipstick: *Walk away or die.*

Taking a couple of steps backward, she stumbled over her overnight bag. She quickly recovered her balance, grabbed her laptop and shoved it inside her small suitcase.

A few seconds later, panting, she was inside her car. She locked the doors and tossed her bag in the back seat. All she could think

about was getting out of there and far away
from Cattle Barge.

But go where?

Chapter Four

Madelyn thumped the steering wheel, refusing to cry. Then the questions flooded. Who was behind this? How did someone find out she was staying at the Red Rope Inn? How on earth did someone get inside her room? Was she being followed? That was a stupid question. Of course someone had followed her—the white sedan from earlier. The feeling of eyes on her prompted her to scrutinize the parking lot.

All the cars appeared to be empty but appearances could be deceiving. She drove around the building to the motel lobby. She parked, locked her car door and stalked inside, tucking her fears as far below the surface as she could. Like a simmering pot, her emotions threatened to boil over without warning.

Later, she would process this horrific day. Right now, all she could think about was finding out who was behind this threat. A dozen scenarios fought for attention. She'd been so quick to blame Owen for trying to run her off the road earlier. Her thoughts moved in a different direction now. The person behind the mirror scrawl was most likely the driver of the white sedan.

It was obvious that someone wanted her far away from Cattle Barge. Did one of Mike Butler's children know about her? What about Ed Staples? Could she trust him? As far as she knew, he was the only one who knew she was coming to the ranch. Why would he summon her there and then try to hurt her? He had her number, probably her home address. Why wouldn't he just assault her without making himself known? It didn't rule him out, but placed him lower on her possible suspect list.

Nothing else made sense. She'd been nearly run off the road, shot at and threatened.

Madelyn was certain of one thing: someone was watching.

A bell jingled as she swung open the glass door to the lobby and stalked inside.

"Where's Trent?" Madelyn asked the smiling woman as she walked to the counter. A metal nametag pinned to her shirt read *Kelsey.*

"Shift change," Kelsey reported, looking a little taken aback by Madelyn's direct question. "How can I help you?"

Madelyn glanced at her watch. One fifteen was an odd time for a shift change. She debated tactics. Being nice usually got her the information she wanted. What had happened back there in her room had thrown her off balance and she felt violated. There was no better way to describe her emotions. She still couldn't figure out who would have an issue with her. The envelope Ed Staples had handed her was sealed. Based on the way he'd examined her features when she'd first arrived and his knowledge of the origin of her mother's necklace, he had to have known the contents. Personally, she didn't know the man from Adam, so she couldn't get a good read on him. Was he a loyal employee to Mike Butler? A personal friend? Or was he closer to the family? Did he feel sorry for them and decide to take matters into his own hands?

He'd seemed honest and even a little bit caring, but maybe it was an act. People faked friendly all the time, smiling at strangers when they were really just trying to get their own way. She'd seen people try to manipulate others using charm tons of times in her line of work. Her profession had also taught her that people had two faces, the one they showed the public and the one they kept to themselves. Both were real. And she could never be certain which one she was getting. Until a tipping point happened…

"Who has access to my room?" Maybe Trent was friends with one of the Butler kids and figured he'd be doing them a favor by scaring her off. That was probably the best-case scenario.

"No one." Kelsey blinked.

"Not even the front office?" Madelyn pressed. Cattle Barge was a small town. If news had leaked that she was the daughter of Mike Butler then someone could be trying to protect the family. Heck, it could've been someone in the family, for all she knew. Was her arrival the tipping point? What about the lawyer reaching out to her? Everyone had to be looked at as a suspect now.

"Well, of course, we have acce—"

"And what about housekeeping?" Madelyn's hands were fisted at her sides as frustration and fear built inside her, gathering steam. What if she'd been in the room? Would that person have attacked?

"Well, yes—"

"Maintenance?"

Kelsey nodded.

"So you and countless others *do* have access to my room." Madelyn was almost to the point of hysterical now. She took in a slow breath that sounded like a hiss from a heating coil.

"Did something happen?" Kelsey caught on. Finally, light brightened her eyes as the insinuation dawned on her.

Part of Madelyn—the frightened child inside her—wanted to deny that any of this was possible. She'd like to write off the whole situation as a bowl of crazy, a landmark bad day. She needed a minute to process the day she was having. More than anything, she needed to hear her father's—well, hold on now, was Charles Kensington even her father anymore?—voice. But that wasn't an option. No matter how many times she phoned, he only returned her calls on the first of every month. Today was the ninth.

Madelyn pulled her cell from her purse. She started punching in those three digits reserved for emergencies. This day had *emergency* stamped all over it.

"Ma'am, what are you doing?" Kelsey asked, her voice low.

"Calling the sheriff," Madelyn stated as she turned her back on the front desk attendant.

"There's no need to do that." Kelsey's voice had that quiet calm as she slowly spoke, drawing out her words like she was trying to talk someone out of jumping off the roof.

"How do you know? I haven't told you why I'm here yet." Madelyn turned toward the glass door in time to see a cruiser pull into the parking lot. He was coming in dark, meaning no lights or sirens.

"I'm sorry. You were so upset and yelling at me, so I hit the panic button my boss had installed under the counter." Now Kelsey sounded nervous.

"Why would I hurt you?" Madelyn heard the irony there. She was being *stalked* and Kelsey had hit the panic button over a few direct words. This time she blew out a slower breath that sounded less like a hiss. "It doesn't matter. Someone broke into my room and I want to file a report anyway. Call and tell them that you hit the button on accident. That we're okay in here."

Silence.

"Kelsey, I'm not in the mood to play games. Would I turn my back to you like this if I was here to hurt you? Make the call." Madelyn swiveled around, hands up. "All I was doing was retrieving my cell so that I could call the sheriff."

Kelsey gave a nervous smile before she picked up the phone.

HUDSON COULDN'T STOP thinking about the stranger, about Madelyn. The sheriff had written the incident off too easily as road rage and hadn't paid enough attention to the fact that she had an angry ex-boyfriend. Even though this wasn't Hudson's business, he put away Bullseye and then climbed into his pickup truck. All he planned to do was drive down to the sheriff's office and put a bug in the man's ear. Sawmill was distracted and anyone could see that he had too much on his plate. Hudson didn't plan to insult the sheriff. He'd find a tactful way to plant the seed about her ex.

Twenty minutes later he was pulling into the parking lot. There was media everywhere and a flock rushed his truck until they got a good look at the driver, realized he wasn't a Butler and dispelled.

He pushed through the mob to the front door, relieved when the lobby was clear. There was a constant hum of chatter from an adjacent room and he suspected that was a "war room" set up

for receiving tips and leads on the Mike Butler murder.

"How are you, Hudson?" Doris asked, rolling her eyes at the craziness going on. She
was midfifties and the type who made it her
personal mission to know what everyone in
town—and in his case, just out of town—was
up to. She was also an old friend of his mother's
before she'd passed away. Lucky for her Hudson's mother had died years before she could
be embarrassed by her son. Hudson performed
a mental headshake. He wasn't there to think
about his own shortcomings and misery.

"Better now that I've had a chance to see
you." The line was cheesy as all get-out but
Doris didn't seem to mind.

She smiled so hard her cheeks turned six
shades past pink.

"And you're a flatterer," she quipped with
that smile intact.

Hudson's gaze drifted to the makeshift command post that had been set up in the adjacent conference room. He heard the buzz of intake volunteers taking calls.

"Looks like you're staying busy." He forced his gaze away from the room and back to Doris. He'd read the stories about Maverick Mike and then Ella Butler.

"Us?" Doris glanced around. "Darn right. This town hasn't seen anything like this in all my considerable years. It's a train wreck in here, if you ask me. I don't remember the last time the sheriff left for more than four hours to sleep. His heart won't take it at this pace."

Pens were lined up in neat rows on her desk next to a line of pencils. She had a notepad positioned on her desk in front of her and her computer was off to one side. A woman like Doris was old-school and would prefer to write things down over spending her days glued to a screen. Hudson was sure she subscribed to the old thinking that staring at the TV too long could make a person go blind.

"Are you trying to convince me that you'd let things get out of control?" He perched on the edge of her desk and she immediately shooed him off it.

"There are other, more qualified people in town who could act as a consultant if they saw fit." The insinuation was that he, being from a big city like Houston, would be more equipped to deal with hard-core crimes, like, say murder. Hudson leaned to one side to avoid the proverbial hand grenade being tossed at him. He had no plans to touch that statement. His days in law enforcement were over.

"What brings you all the way into town?" She blinked her eyes up at him like she was ready for him to tell her the sky was falling.

"Can't I check on my favorite person once in a while?" He wasn't ready to tip his hand. Gauging from the chaos in the office, the sheriff didn't have the resources to properly address the reporter's incident. And that worried Hudson for reasons he shouldn't care about. He'd done his part, played the role of Good Samaritan. If he had any sense he'd turn around, walk out that door and let a sleeping dog alone.

Instead, he took a seat across from Doris and leaned forward.

"Thanks for the habanero peppers, by the way. Diced some up and threw them in the pan with a pair of eggs this morning. Best breakfast I've had in months," he said.

"There's something about homegrown that gives 'em that extra kick of flavor." Her eyes lit up. His mom used to joke that her friend grew a garden in small part to feed herself and in large part so that she could stop by and check on her friends on a regular basis. "If you'd come around more often, I'd send you home with all you want. I always grow more than I can use in case someone's in need."

"Now I'm a charity case?" Hudson joked but a pang of guilt nailed him. He'd been content to stick to his ranch. Heck, he'd have his groceries delivered if it meant never leaving his property. The place was the only thing keeping him sane after everything he'd lost and he'd pretty much lost everything.

Once again, he had to ask himself why he was sitting in the sheriff's office.

"Is the boss around?" He glanced toward the hallway.

"Afraid not. Everything all right?" Concern creased her forehead.

"With me? Yeah. I was just checking on a friend," he said.

"Since when do you have a friend in town?" Her brow shot up.

The phone rang. She excused herself to take the call.

Hudson had almost talked himself into slipping out the door while she was preoccupied with the conversation. Until he heard her say the name Madelyn Kensington.

"Where is she?" Doris asked.

Hudson leaned a little closer to Doris's desk.

"The Red Rope Inn, got it," she said low into the receiver. "I'll sure tell the sheriff when he returns. Should be half an hour or so."

Did something happen to Madelyn?

"She's hysterical? What about?" Doris asked into the phone. "Okay. I got it. I'll let him know. Thank you for the call." Before Doris could end her conversation and delay Hudson with questions, he was out the door.

Madelyn was in trouble. He'd heard it in Doris's voice. The Red Rope Inn was eighteen minutes from there, according to his GPS device. He glanced at the route, confident he could make it in ten.

Hudson zipped in and out of cars. The deputy on duty wouldn't appreciate any interference with his investigation, so Hudson needed to think of a good excuse to show up. Mentioning Doris might get her in trouble, and based on his proximity, he had about two minutes to come up with a plausible excuse.

The parking lot was quiet. All the action was going on inside the lobby, Hudson noticed as he searched for Madelyn through the glass. His pulse calmed a notch when he saw her—saw that she was okay—and he didn't want to care as much as he did. He told himself it was the action he missed and not the person who'd occupied his thoughts since she'd driven away.

"I couldn't get ahold of you on your cell." He made a beeline toward Madelyn with the pretense they were a couple. The bell gave away his presence the second the door moved.

Her gaze flew to him and he couldn't immediately discern if his being there was a good thing or not.

"Why are you here?" The shock in her voice gave away the answer...not thrilled.

Chapter Five

Deputy Hank Harley stepped in between Hudson and Madelyn, blocking the path. The deputy's left hand came up, palm aimed at Hudson, and his right remained firmly on the butt of his Glock. He was ready for that split-second decision that might come where he had to pull his weapon and fire. The action was so automatic that most cops kept a hand on their gun even during what many would consider routine traffic stops. Officers knew that traffic stops were right up there with domestic disturbance calls in terms of threat to an officer's safety. Hudson didn't know Harley on a personal level. He'd done his best to keep his presence as quiet as possible since returning to Cattle Barge a year ago, which meant Harley didn't know him or his background. That could be dangerous if Hudson charged in like a bull, so he stopped and made sure his hands were visible to the deputy.

"I'm going to have to ask you to leave, sir." Harley took a step toward Hudson. Most would view the move as threatening. A law-enforcement officer had one primary goal when he left for work—make it home again. Hudson appreciated Harley's motivation. But he was on a mission, too. *Tread lightly.*

"I'm a friend. I just want to make sure she's okay." Both hands went up to show he wasn't carrying a weapon. Texas was open-carry and that put some people on edge.

Harley sidestepped, putting Hudson and Madelyn in his line of sight, and he looked like he was seeking confirmation from Madelyn.

"I can use a friend right now." She didn't ask

the obvious question: How did he know she was there?

Hudson took her encouragement as a good sign.

"What's going on?" he asked, careful not to infringe on Harley's investigation. Any random person who cared about a victim would ask the same question.

"Someone was inside my room and left a message for me." Her eyes were wild. She didn't need to spell it out for him. He immediately realized she'd been threatened. He also noted how exhausted she looked. He ignored the inappropriate stir of attraction, chalking it up to overprotective instincts. Yeah, right. He was being chivalrous and that was all those feelings were. He couldn't sell water in the desert with a fake sales pitch like that. But this wasn't the time to worry about it.

"The white sedan?" Hudson took a purposeful stride toward her and the deputy didn't protest, which was the second good sign since he'd arrived.

"That's what I'm trying to ascertain," Harley said as Madelyn released a panicked-sounding sigh.

"I'm not sure. I mean, I guess. The person from the sedan makes sense. I didn't see anyone coming and going from the parking lot." The words rushed out all at once, almost sounding like they were tripping over each other.

"Is there surveillance video of the parking lot?" Hudson moved to her side without protest from Harley. He expected to maybe put a hand on her shoulder to provide some sense of comfort but she shot up and practically pounced toward him. He had to catch her to stop her from crashing into him and she immediately buried her face in his chest.

"I'm sorry." She pulled back after his muscles went rigid.

"It's fine." The feel of her body against his

sent a lightning bolt directly to the center of his chest. Not usually the reaction he had with a woman this close but this wasn't the time to break it apart. He pushed the feeling aside as she leaned her head against his chest. His heart pounded and he told himself that it was from the rush of adrenaline that accompanied the possibility of real action and not from physical contact with her.

"There's no video on that side of the lot," the motel worker said.

"I'll check footage of nearby sites," the deputy said.

They both knew that could take days. Hudson thanked Harley anyway.

The deputy told everyone to stay put before he excused himself, presumably to check out her room.

"What did the message say?" There was no way Harley was going to let Hudson trample all over his crime scene, so he'd have to rely on Madelyn. She was trained to look for things out of the ordinary, same as him. But she was flustered and it was her life on the line and that made a difference.

"That I should walk away or die. It was scribbled on the mirror and I have no idea how anyone got inside. I mean, I sure didn't let anyone in my room or leave the door unlocked. You're the only person I know in town." She flashed her eyes at him, sending another jolt of electricity straight to his chest. Being this close to her was like standing on live wires in a thunderstorm.

"I'm guessing the staff denies giving out a key." He glanced toward the clerk.

"Yes. In fact, she's the one who called the law *on me*." Another flash of those cornflower blue eyes. She was scared but there was a lot more going on and he couldn't pinpoint what else it was. Exhaustion…yes. Fear…absolutely. Desperation…and another emotion…

"So far today someone ran you off the road and presumably another person has threatened you?" he asked.

"That about sums it up," she stated, and he didn't like the defeat in her voice.

"Did the deputy give you any indication of whether or not he believed the two incidents were related?" he continued.

"He said that it all seemed suspect and like it could be connected," she answered. There might be defeat in her voice but there was defiance in her eyes.

"*Could* be?" Hudson scoffed.

The bell on the door jingled.

"I'm afraid we should go into the station," the deputy said to Madelyn, and Hudson didn't like the way Harley looked at her.

"Oh, okay." She didn't seem to catch on to the fact this wasn't a good sign.

"My friend here is tired. She's had a long day." Hudson wanted to feel out the deputy.

He glanced at his watch. "It's long past dinner time. She's probably starving, so I was thinking that I could bring her by after we grab a bite."

"I can give her a ride. It shouldn't take long for her to answer a few more questions," Harley said.

"Is there a good reason why I can't answer them right here?" She seemed to be catching on to Hudson's hesitation because her brow hiked up.

Harley didn't immediately answer.

"Can I ask a question, Deputy?" Hudson took a step closer to Harley and lowered his voice.

"Yes, sir," Harley said. Back with the "sir" business. What had changed in the last few minutes?

"What did you find in her room?" Hudson made sure his voice was low enough that only Harley could hear.

"Nothing," the deputy said. "Absolutely nada."

MADELYN STRAINED TO hear what Hudson was saying to the deputy and couldn't. It would be difficult to hear anything over the sound of her racing pulse. Yes, because it had been one hell of a day. But also because of the handsome cowboy in the room and it was totally inappropriate to think about that right now. So, she pushed those unproductive thoughts aside.

"What did he say?" she asked as Hudson walked toward her.

His shrug wasn't the most reassuring.

"Are you hungry?" he asked.

"I doubt I could eat anything," she stated.

"He wants you to ride with him to the station." His look of sympathy confused her.

"Why?" But she really wanted to ask why the cowboy was looking at her like she might be a little crazy.

"Because he wants to evaluate your statement and ask the same questions a few different ways to see if he can trip you up." An apologetic look followed but she appreciated his honesty.

"So he either thinks I'm a wack-job or..."

It hit her fast and hard like a bomb dropping out of the sky on a clear summer day.

"He thinks I'm guilty of something? Like what? Why would I scribble a threat on my own mirror?" She glared at the deputy now, putting him in the same category as the front desk clerk. This day was off-the-chain bad. What on earth had she done to deserve such awful luck recently? First, she'd been dealing with a bad breakup. Okay, "bad" was calling it lightly. Then she'd learned that her father might not be her... Never mind... She couldn't even go there right now. In the process of receiving the most earth-shattering news of her life, Madelyn had been run off the road and now her life had been threatened. That should be the worst of it, but, no, this day had somehow managed to get even worse as the deputy suspected *her* of doing something. But what? Yelling at the front desk clerk wasn't exactly a crime.

"There's nothing in your room," Hudson said.

"What do you mean?" She didn't quite absorb those words. "Of course there is. It's written plain as day on the mirror."

Hudson shook his head.

Hold on…

Madelyn knew exactly what that meant.

"What are you doing in *here* when the wack-job who threatened me is out *there*?" she asked the deputy, her anger rising to the surface and bubbling over. "The person who did this is probably right outside staring at us this very second and you're in here…what?…thinking that I'm nuts?"

Hudson seemed to be on the same page because he was already at the window, scanning the area, and she assumed that he was searching for whoever was behind this. Someone was messing with her, that much was clear.

Ed Staples?

He seemed to know all about her paternity and that was what this was all about. Wasn't it? Being run off the road. The threat. Someone had tried to keep her from coming to town, and now that she was here, that same person wanted her to leave quietly.

"Ma'am, if you don't mind. I'd like to get to the sheriff's office so we can clear all this up." The deputy's body was angled toward her. "We'll send someone to analyze the scene and they'll find the truth."

He didn't exactly say "crime scene." If Kelsey hadn't hit the panic button, Madelyn doubted he would've shown up at all.

"Am I under arrest?" she asked point-black.

"No, ma'am."

"Then no. I won't go to the station with you."

Madelyn knew her rights and she didn't have to put up with any of this.

Hudson spun around, and when his attention was directed at her, frissons of heat rippled through her. "You sure about that?"

"I have no intention of running around in circles with a deputy—or anyone else, for that matter—who doesn't believe me," she said. "Call the sheriff. He'll be able to tell you what happened earlier with a white sedan. That couldn't have been in my imagination because the man standing near you witnessed the whole scene. I'm being followed, targeted, and I'm tired of playing games. I already told you what happened here and you can believe me or not. It's your choice. But I'm walking out that door and getting into my own car unless my hands are zip-cuffed."

"Stay in town where I can reach you," the deputy said. She knew enough about the law to realize he had nothing to hold her on. Asking her to go down to the station with him was ridiculous. What would they do there anyway? The place was overrun, and when she really looked at him, the deputy had dark circles cradling his eyes. He was most likely overworked and overwrought, and since he couldn't tell that a crime had been committed, he was grasping at straws.

"Do you know of any hotels where I'll be safe?" She shot an intentional look at Kelsey.

"I have a place in mind." The cowboy stood, feet apart, in an athletic stance. He was almost intimidatingly tall, and a trill of awareness skittered across her skin as she noticed. "My ranch. You can stay with me until this is sorted out."

She wanted to argue against the idea, but, honestly, she was too tired to put up much of a fight. Exhaustion wore her nerves thin, and questions about her family, her heritage, pecked at her skull. But being with Hudson 24/7? Was that really such a good idea?

"You have a problem with the arrangement?" she asked the deputy. Madelyn was still undecided but she couldn't think of a better option.

"I guess not," Harley responded.

If he couldn't come up with an objection, neither could she. So, that had to be a good thing. Right?

"TELL ME EVERYTHING that happened," Hudson said as he poured a fresh cup of coffee and then handed it to Madelyn. Being back in his kitchen was odd, considering she'd known him less than a day. Rather than analyze it after what had become one of the longest days of her life, she tucked it aside.

The mug warmed her hands and she welcomed the burn on her throat with the first sip.

He already knew the details of the road incident. Then there was the news about Mike

Butler, but there was no way she planned to talk about something she had yet to verify or understand. *Although, it could be significant*, a little voice in the back of her mind said.

Madelyn sized up Hudson. Should she really bare her soul to a man who was keeping his identity a secret? She'd had her fill of deceptions for one day. Check that, for one lifetime. Everything she thought she knew could be a lie. This man was a rancher about as much as she was a sous-chef. To be clear, the only thing she knew how to make in the kitchen was toast, and there were no guarantees she wouldn't burn the bread. She could, however, make a mean cup of coffee thanks to pods and machines that basically did all the work.

"I can tell what you're thinking," he said and his voice startled her. "Don't lie to me or hide anything."

"I'm sure I have no idea what you mean," she said lamely. He seemed to know that she was evaluating him, trying to decide if she should ask about his background. Strangers confided in her all the time courtesy of her line of work. But this guy? Everything about his posture said he was a closed book.

So, how could she put her faith in someone who didn't trust her?

Chapter Six

Chapter Six

"Do you remember anything about the driver of the sedan that you didn't think of earlier?" Hudson asked Madelyn. She'd been sizing him up while they made small talk and he needed to see if she'd decided to trust him. *Trust* might be a strong word. *Confide* was better.

"No. I couldn't get a good look at his face because of the ski mask," she admitted.

"Which no one wears in Texas, let alone on a day with hundred-degree heat," he stated.

"I didn't notice any white cars in the parking lot, and after this morning I've been watching for that guy to return." She rolled the coffee mug in between her palms before adding, "There were two trucks and a minivan when I arrived."

Hudson had hoped that the coffee would bring some color back to her face. She was still white and her lips purple from a little bit of shock and a healthy dose of fear. "I like that you were watching out for the driver to return. You mentioned a boyfriend before, a bad breakup. Are you still thinking in that direction?"

For a split second her lips thinned, forming a small line.

"Wish I could be sure," she said with a shrug.

What was she holding back? "Why else would a random person want to rattle you or force you to leave town?"

"What makes you think this guy doesn't want me dead?" The whites of her eyes shone brightly against the fluorescent lights in his kitchen.

"My first thought is—" He flashed his eyes

at her. "Forgive my bluntness, but he could've shot you on the road."

"True."

"So, this person is worried about hurting innocent people," he said.

"Or he was waiting for a clean shot," she stated.

Okay, he'd give her that, so he nodded. He took another sip of coffee and let the thought simmer. "He might've been trying to scare you."

"Mission accomplished," she said on a harsh sigh.

Why would someone try to scare her? Did the driver assume she hadn't learned her lesson after he'd tried to run her off the road? Did he follow her to the motel, break in and scribble the message once she left? Those actions indicated someone trying to scare her, not kill her. But scare her away from what? Experience had taught him that deep down the victim knew.

The trick to breaking open an investigation was helping her realize it.

"Why did you say you were going to Hereford Ranch?" he questioned.

"I didn't."

Hudson took in a sharp breath. "I thought you wanted my help."

"You offered protection and I took it. Not the same thing." She didn't break eye contact. "Can I ask you a question?"

He nodded.

"Why do you care?"

"I don't," he said, selling the lie with a stone-cold glare.

Her shoulders stiffened and she gave as good as she got in the icy-stare department.

Hudson ought to be grateful that she was throwing him a lifeline with the cold-shoulder routine because he was sliding down a slippery slope. He didn't want to give a hoot what happened to her—hell, to anyone. And he considered himself smart enough to pull back when he realized he was fighting a losing battle.

But that look she shot him stung.

And a deep need to break down a few of her walls welled up. For reasons he wouldn't dissect or fight, he stalked toward her. He stopped inches from her. She was shorter than him by almost a foot and had the most delicate lines on her face. His fingers flexed and released as her hand came up to his chest as if to stop him. Instead of pushing him back a step like he assumed she would, she grabbed a fistful of his T-shirt and tugged him toward her. Those gorgeous blue eyes of hers were staring up at him, daring him to take this a step further.

This close, the pull was too much to ignore. So, he dipped his head and kissed her. The taste of coffee was still on her lips.

Hudson braced himself for the rejection he expected to come but didn't. Instead of shoving him away, she drew him closer and parted her lips. He drove his tongue inside her mouth and tasted the sweet mix of her and the bold coffee.

Her hands, which had been fisted in his shirt, released the material before planting on his shoulders. There was so much heat in that one kiss Hudson almost had to take a step back to absorb the blast. He didn't. And so they stood, toe to toe, tongues engaged.

He brought his right hand up to her neck, his thumb resting on the base where her pulse pounded wildly, matching the tempo of his own. With one small forward step the gap between them disappeared. That one move, seemingly so insignificant, was gasoline-poured-onto-a-fire hot. The air crackled around them with the intensity of burning embers.

The kiss, meant to build a bridge of trust, had knocked Hudson completely off balance. Right, extending an olive branch. That was all he was doing and not satisfying a primal urge he'd felt since he first set eyes on her.

Whatever his motive, the earth shifted underneath his feet and his heart shot a warning flare. Keep this up; get into serious trouble.

Pulling back was difficult but necessary. Looking at those pink lips when he did was a mistake but one he made anyway. Hell, why not? He was racking up errors in judgment today. What was one more?

"That shouldn't have happened," he said sternly. She looked at him like she wasn't sure whom he was trying to convince, him or her.

"It won't again," she said with similar conviction.

"Back to the case." He took a step back and searched the countertop for his cup of coffee, thinking that he liked the taste of it on her tongue better. Somewhere along the way, he'd set his mug down but couldn't remember when or where for the life of him. He spied it next to where he stood before the kiss—a kiss that he tried to convince himself meant nothing. Tell that to the beating lump in his chest, hammering wildly against his ribs.

Hudson topped off his mug and took a sip. "Where were we?"

"I was about to tell you something that can't leave this room." Madelyn didn't meet his gaze this time as he examined her.

Difficult truths were more easily admitted sitting down, so he led her to the round table off the kitchen.

She sat there for a minute and he didn't speak. She seemed to be pulling on all her strength to say what was on her mind and he had no plans to intrude. This was the look victims got before they told their stories. Hudson's stomach lining twisted thinking about her in those terms. He didn't like thinking of her in any way other than the strong, capable and intelligent woman she was.

"Ed Staples is Mike Butler's attorney. He summoned me to Cattle Barge with the prom-

ise of telling me something I'd want to know."
Her voice was even and it seemed to be taking
all her energy to keep it that way as she stared
out the window. "I thought he was going to
give me a scoop, you know, an exclusive. In
hindsight, I guess I should've realized that I
was being set up."

She stilled and Hudson didn't so much as
make a sound. Frighten her away now and she
might disappear into the woods like a hunted
deer, and never return. For reasons Hudson
didn't want to examine, he needed to know
why Ed Staples had contacted her.

A sharp sigh pealed from her lips before she
continued. "What I'm about to tell you hasn't
been confirmed, or, at least, I haven't had any
tests run to prove or disprove it."

Hudson nodded encouragement for her to
continue. She needed the space to do that on
her own terms, so he patiently waited with his
eyes cast down.

"And it can't leave this room. I mean, it will get out eventually and will be big news, but I need your word that you'll keep this between us for now," she stated.

"You have it," he responded, making eye contact. She needed to know how seriously he took his promises.

"Basically, if I'm to believe Ed Staples then Maverick Mike Butler is my father." Madelyn crossed her arms tightly. Her shoulders tensed. Muscles around her eyes tightened. Looking at her, it was like a wall was coming up between them. Her face lost expression and he understood that she was distancing herself from what might be the truth, like he'd seen so many victims do while recounting their stories.

The admission sat in the air between them, too thick to wade through at the moment. Money always topped the list of motives. Greed ranked right up there with crime-of-passion killings. Based on her expression while telling him the news, she hadn't seen any of this coming. She was telling him now because she obviously believed someone wasn't happy with this revelation. A good reporter would easily clue into motivation. "Who knows about this?"

"Besides the two of us?" The blank stare overshadowed all the heat and intensity that had been on her face only moments ago. It was like she'd faded out. A washed-out version of her sat in front of him as though someone had scrubbed all the vibrancy and color out of her face. And yet she was still beautiful.

Hudson nodded.

"Ed Staples."

"STAPLES, THE BUTLER family attorney, summoned you to Cattle Barge to tell you Mike Butler is your father?" Hudson asked, and she shared the shock on his face that he quickly tried to cover.

"Yes."

"On your way to receive the news someone runs you off the road." He seemed to be thinking out loud because he was staring at his coffee mug. "And then—what?—you come back to your room to a threatening message."

"That's right," she admitted.

"My question is simple. Why not shoot when the driver had the chance?" Hudson pushed his chair back from the table and leaned forward, his elbows resting on his knees.

"I wondered the same thing." She shrugged.

"Let's go back to the beginning. When I first met you there was a possibility that your ex was behind this. Is there any way, in your mind, he could be involved?" His gaze came up to meet hers and she had to fight with everything inside her not to give away how tenuous her hold on her emotions was. The tether, however small, attaching her to logic and reason was a lifeline she couldn't afford to snap.

"What would he have to gain?" she asked.

"Good question. For now, we'll set him aside as a suspect." He took a sip of coffee before setting his mug on the table. "I need to talk to Ed Staples."

"I doubt it's him. He knew my phone number, and my address was right there on the letter he gave me. Why call me in the first place? I mean, if he wanted to get rid of me I would've never seen it coming. My guess is that someone besides the three of us knows about this… *possibility*." She didn't bother to hide the frustration in her voice. It wouldn't do any good. The life she'd known for thirty years was over if this was true. Then again, wouldn't it be just like a self-centered billionaire to lie about something just to manipulate the lives of others? But what good would that do now that he was gone? "Before I do anything else, I need confirmation that he's my father."

"Ed Staples didn't provide proof?" His brow shot up.

"I have no plans to take someone else's word on it. I'll need a few days to arrange testing on my terms. I'm not even sure how to go about it yet, so I have to do a little research first," she continued. A little seed of hope that this could all be a bad dream was blossoming somewhere deep inside her.

"What about your mother? Can you ask her?"

"She died when I was born, so, no." The sadness in her voice caught her off guard. Her hand came up absently to toy with the dragonfly necklace. If Mike Butler was her father that meant she knew even less about her mother. Her father had made the subject off-limits, but the knowledge her mother had died because of negligent hospital practices had driven so many of Madelyn's choices. She didn't need Freud to tell her why she'd taken a job as an investigative reporter. She wanted to give answers, peace, to other families. She wanted others to avoid dangerous situations being covered up by hospitals, businesses and crooks. She wanted to protect people from the kind of pain she'd experienced.

"I'm sorry," Hudson said quietly with a gentleness that threatened to crack the wall Madelyn had built to protect herself.

"It's all I've ever known, so..." There had been countless times in her life that she'd wished for her mother. When she was a little girl she used to imagine what it would be like to have a real mom for a few hours, days, years. Madelyn had played the what-she-would-trade game more times than she could count. There were times when she would've traded years from her own life for just a few minutes with the woman. Madelyn had grown up believing her mother had been a saint. She'd built the woman up to angelic status. From a child's eyes, her mother could do no wrong, and she'd carried that belief into adulthood. So, this betrayal hurt like hell and a piece of her still wanted to cling to the fantasy where her mother was perfect.

A thought struck—a dark thought—and the devastation must've shown on her face because Hudson scooted his chair toward her and took one of her hands in his.

"What is it?" he asked.

"I was just wondering if my father knew that I might not be his biological child. Or did my mother have an affair and hide the truth?" A tear escaped because it would explain so much about their relationship. The cowboy thumbed it away. Contact caused her stomach to quiver.

Of course, if her father—could she even still call him that until she knew one way or the other?—had known the truth, it could be the reason he'd kept her at arm's length all these years. Did he resent her for not being his child? For causing her mother to die?

"Is he…?" Hudson didn't seem to want to finish the sentence, so she did it for him.

"Dead? No. He's very much alive." If she could call it that. He maintained the same boring routine since she could remember—up by 5:00 a.m., breakfast, work until after 7:30 p.m., dinner. Bed. Sundays, he worked around the yard and stayed in the garage most of the day.

"But you don't want to ask him?" That brow arched again.

"It's complicated." She blew out a breath.

"So, we focus on who stands to lose if you stick around," he said, and she was thankful that he'd redirected the conversation.

She'd have to deal with her emotions later, and if the revelation was true, she figured she'd be dealing with them on some level for the rest of her life. How did anyone process or reconcile a deception of that scale? Her entire identity had been shattered the minute Ed Staples had handed her that letter.

Madelyn's cell buzzed and the noise made

her jump. She scanned the countertops for her purse. Where had she set it down?

"The racket is coming from over here," Hudson said, making a move to get up.

"I got it." The words came out more sharply than she'd intended. "Sorry."

Hudson didn't respond as he gripped his mug and refilled his coffee.

Madelyn located her phone and glanced at the screen. She had six text messages from her ex.

"Everything okay?" Hudson asked.

"Yeah. Fine."

"I've come to learn that word means just the opposite. I take it the messages are from someone you're not anxious to hear from," he said. He leaned against the counter as he studied her face.

She didn't want to be under scrutiny right now. Exhaustion made it difficult to fake a smile, let alone lift up the phone.

"Are you hungry?" he asked.

"Don't go to any trouble," she said. "I doubt I could eat anything anyway."

"I'm not much in the kitchen but I can throw something on the grill. Won't take half an hour and that'll give you time to clean up and rest before supper," he said.

"A shower does sound amazing right now," she offered and under normal circumstances would've enjoyed the quick glance of appreciation. He'd kissed her before but that was most likely to keep her from becoming hysterical. But an attraction? Her body reacted to him every time he was close, and even though they couldn't act on it, she felt satisfied to know that he was having a similar reaction to her.

He was, right?

Or was she just seeing something she wanted to see?

After her relationship with Owen had gone the way it had, she wasn't feeling the most confident in her decision-making ability when it came to the opposite sex. Besides, she'd touched the stove. Been burned. And had no plans to step into the kitchen anytime soon, not even for a man who made her pulse pound wildly by just being in the same room with her.

Besides, she didn't even know the cowboy beyond the surface and a simmering attraction. And her life had just been turned upside down, which was probably why she was fabricating a relationship in her mind with him when she needed to take a step back so she could sort out the craziness.

The worst part?

She was still thinking about how right the world had felt when he pressed his lips to hers and all the background noise disappeared.

"Madelyn?" The cowboy's voice was low, concerned, like if he spoke too loudly he might startle her.

He did and she jumped anyway, quickly reining in her emotions.

"Forensics will most likely find a print in your room and this will be cleared up before you know it," he said. "You're welcome to stay here as long as you need to, but if you stand in that spot much longer I'm going to be tempted to kiss you again."

"Which way did you say the shower was?" she asked.

He pointed to the hallway behind her.

Scooping up her overnight bag, she spun around and marched toward it.

Every ranch-style house she'd been in had the same layout, so she'd only asked to test if she could trust her voice. Because she wanted the cowboy's lips on hers again. But wanting and doing were two different things and she needed to keep a clear head.

It was most likely the stress of the day that had her wanting to feel his big strong hands on her again, roaming her body and getting to know every inch of her.

Or something else that she couldn't afford to consider. Something that had her gripping her bag and trying to decide if she should march into that kitchen or go against every urge inside her and force herself into the bathroom.

Madelyn released the bag, causing it to tumble onto the floor. Then she stalked into the next room.

Chapter Seven

A cold shower went a long way toward cooling Madelyn's skin and helping her refocus. She toweled off and moved into the adjacent bedroom.

She could tell that Hudson wasn't kidding about his grilling skills, based on the smells wafting down the hall while she dressed. Freshly brushed teeth and clean clothes had her feeling like her old self again. *Almost.* A part of her wondered if she'd ever be that person again.

Since going down that road before she had proof was as productive as trying to take notes using a dead branch, she checked her cell. Still no calls from her father and there was an odd comfort in that fact. Well, she guessed he was still her father. What if he wasn't? If Mike Butler was her biological father she had no one left: both of her parents would be dead. She seriously doubted his four children would be thrilled by her presence. Heck, one or all of them could be behind the threat. The guy in the white sedan could've followed her to the motel, written the note when she was on her way to the ranch. The Butlers could've hired someone to chase her away.

Madelyn didn't realize how tightly she'd been gripping her phone until she caught a glimpse of her knuckles, which were bone-white. On a deep intake of air, she pushed off the bed and strode into the kitchen.

"Steaks are ready," Hudson said.

On the table were two plates of steaks, grilled asparagus and mushrooms, along with what looked like hash brown potatoes. So, he was gorgeous *and* could cook. Most women would consider they'd hit the jackpot if a man like him made dinner, and normally she would, too. Now, however, Madelyn's thoughts couldn't stray far from her circumstances.

"Didn't have enough time to bake those." He motioned toward the plate containing the potatoes.

"Are you kidding? Hash browns are my favorite," she said with more enthusiasm than she'd expected. "Sorry, I must be hungrier than I realized."

"You're kidding, right? Because I know you didn't just apologize for appreciating what I cooked," he said with a smile that could seduce a room full of women with one flash. Her included, based on the way her heart fluttered.

She needed to keep that in mind and her emotions in check because an attraction with a man who kept secrets was right up there with asking to be tied up and thrown in the ocean. "Do you normally have two steaks ready to go?"

"Not usually, no." He motioned toward the table, for her to take a seat as he pulled her chair out for her.

And then it dawned on her that he'd been expecting company. Of course he would be. He was gorgeous and with that voice—a deep rumble with just enough cadence to let her know he was full-blooded Texan. His name seemed familiar, she realized now, but she couldn't place the reason and half figured her imagination was at work.

"I'm sorry if I messed up your plans," she quickly added with an apologetic look as her cheeks flamed. He was being kind but he had a life and probably someone special. The thought struck her as odd that this stranger knew so much about her and she knew very little about him. She glanced around the room, looking for any signs of a female presence; a man as good-looking as Hudson must have a girlfriend.

"No problem." He wasn't giving up a whole lot, either.

Madelyn sat at the table, unsure she'd be able to eat half of her plate, so she surprised herself when fifteen minutes later the entire plate was clear.

"You didn't say much during dinner." He motioned toward the plate. "I'm guessing the steak was okay."

"Better than that. It was amazing." Her stomach was happy, the kind of happy that came with a satisfying meal. Being with the strong, capable cowboy settled her nerves enough to relax. The smile he gave warmed her in places she couldn't afford to allow. Those were a few more things she didn't need to notice about the mysterious man.

He cleared his plate.

"At least let me do the dishes," she protested.

"Not tonight. This meal is on me," he said with the smile that carved out dimples in both cheeks.

"I'd like to contribute in some way." Madelyn had learned early on that there was no such thing as a free meal.

"How about making breakfast tomorrow morning? Can you handle that?" he asked.

She shrugged. "I can try. But I'm better at cleaning up afterward."

The deep rumble that started in his chest and rolled out was pretty darn sexy. It took a second to register that he was laughing at her.

"What did I say that was so funny?" she asked, a little indignant.

"It was the look on your face at the suggestion of cooking, like I'd just asked you to lick the bottom of my boot," he said with more of that rumble.

"You may not want to eat anything that comes from a kitchen where I'm in charge," she said.

"So I gathered," he said before his expression changed. "While you were in the shower, I checked in with the sheriff's office."

"Oh, yeah? What did he have to say?" Madelyn took her plate to the sink.

"He apologized on behalf of his deputy. I don't need to remind you how overworked they are over there with everything else going on." Hudson motioned for her to hand it over.

"That's not exactly reassuring," she stated honestly.

"It does make you a lot less safe than I'd like," he agreed. "But you're fine as long as you're here."

She handed over the plate. It was time to fold. Besides, she might not be alive if it weren't for the chivalrous cowboy. "Thank you, by the way. Not just for dinner and giving me a place to stay tonight, but for everything you've done so far."

He shrugged off her comment. His kindness

might not be much to him. She figured helping a woman in distress was part of his code. But it meant everything to her. He seemed like a decent guy and she was pretty certain that he was her only friend in town.

Beyond the obvious, she knew very little about him. A shiver raced through her as she searched her memory to see if there'd been a lock on the bedroom door.

"Coffee?" he asked.

"I'd love some but you have to let me get it." She shot him a severe look as he started to wave her off again. "It'll make me feel better about your hospitality if you let me do something for you."

A smile parted his lips and her thoughts immediately zeroed in on the kiss they'd shared earlier. So much heat and…what else?… temptation.

Well, she really didn't need to go there. Her thoughts immediately snapped to Owen, and the emotional burns were still fresh. She refilled their mugs from earlier, trying to push thoughts of her ex out of her mind. Those seemed, she didn't know, out of place while spending time with Hudson.

He thanked her as he took the mug, and sparks lit when their fingers brushed against each other.

"I can't say that I know much about Mike Butler's family." She reclaimed her seat at the table.

"He has four kids that I know of." He shot an apologetic look toward her before adding, "Possibly five but we haven't confirmed that yet."

"I remember reading something about them. There's a set of twins, male. And two females," she said, ignoring the pounding in her chest. She was grateful the cowboy hadn't lumped her in as family. Until she had definitive proof, she had no plans to call herself a Butler. The thought did cross her mind that Mike Butler could've afforded the best medical care on the planet for her mother. Had he known at the time that Madelyn was his? Anger roared through her at the possibility and her hand came up to the necklace for reassurance. She fingered the detail.

"Everything okay?" Hudson asked, shaking her out of her heavy thoughts.

"Yes, sure. We were talking about the Butlers," she said.

"That's right. Ella Butler's the oldest and Cadence is the youngest. Of course, there've been a couple of people claiming to belong to the Butler clan." His one eyebrow arched as he watched her. "Time will tell."

"Well, I'm not one of them," she stated a little too tartly. She started to apologize but he waved her off like it was no big deal. It was. She wasn't normally so rude to someone trying to help her. "It's not okay to come off as a jerk. I've had too much coming at me and I'm still processing."

"It's a lot," he admitted, and she was grateful someone understood. She was clueless as to what to do with the information. Even if she could get ahold of her father to ask what he knew, how would she even approach the subject?

Excuse me, Dad...but are you really my dad? Or, *Did you know Mom was cheating on you?*

Was he from here? "Do you know the Butlers personally?"

"Only from the news, which I don't pay much attention to." He took another sip of coffee before setting the cup on the table.

More questions pecked at her skull and there was no chance of getting answers tonight. At this rate, she'd end the night with a raging headache and that was about all.

"Have you lived here long?" She needed to

think about something else to give herself a break.

"Not really."

"Did you grow up here?" Madelyn wanted to know more about Hudson and, let's face it, she wanted to talk about something besides her crazy day for a change.

He drained his cup and stood. "You've already seen your bedroom and you know where the bathroom is. If you need more towels or blankets, you'll find them in the hall closet. I like to run the AC when I sleep. That's all you need to know to get through the night."

With that, he walked away.

Okay. Madelyn rinsed out both cups. She glanced around, looking for something that would tell her more about Hudson Dale. The place seemed normal enough. Even though there weren't many decorations, the few he had were simple and well-placed. She heard the shower turn on in the other room and forced thoughts of him undressing out of her mind. This day had been out of control and the last thing she needed to do was let her imagination run wild. It was her imagination that made her good at her job. She was able to come at a topic from every angle until she fit all the puzzle pieces together. But that same imagination had her wondering if she'd be okay alone in a stranger's house.

Madelyn almost laughed out loud. She knew the statistics. A woman's greatest threat came from those she knew and, in most cases, loved. She found the notion that she'd be safest with a complete stranger ironic. It was true, though.

Even so, she checked her bedroom door for a lock and was disappointed when she didn't find one. After brushing her teeth, she glanced around the room, looking for anything to secure the door closed. The dresser was a heavy wood piece, significant, and probably too heavy to move on her own. The chair in the corner could work. She repositioned the back underneath the door handle like she'd seen done countless times in movies. Call her crazy but her day had been right up there with one of her worst and, bad as it had been, could get worse if she let her guard down.

A ridiculous part of her said she'd been in way more trouble when she'd locked lips with the handsome cowboy. He threatened to bring a part of her to life that no one before him had.

MADELYN FINALLY UNDERSTOOD what it meant to sleep with one eye open. That wasn't entirely true because she didn't actually sleep. Instead, she drifted in and out, half expecting someone to burst through the door at any second. The night could best be described as fits and starts, and she'd almost thrown in the towel half a dozen times. Relief washed over her when the sun finally peeked through the slats in the mini-blinds and she could get up without disturbing her host.

Her mind kept spinning over the previous day and her possible parentage.

A soft knock at the door came about the time she sat up. She pulled the covers up to her chin as her pulse galloped.

"Coffee's ready," the strong male voice belonging to Hudson said. The sound made her heart stutter.

"I'll be right out." Her gaze flew to her body, making sure every inch of her skin was covered below the chin. And that was silly when she thought about it because he was on the other side of a closed door. Emotion had momentarily overtaken logic. If this was any indication of how well her brain was going to work today, Madelyn was in for a real treat.

She stretched sore muscles, dressed and threw her hair up in a ponytail, trying to bring herself back to center with deep breathing techniques she'd learned in yoga class in college. When that didn't work, she decided she needed caffeine. Like, now. Or sooner.

"Morning," Hudson said, looking fresh as she made a beeline for the coffeepot.

"Same," she grumbled. She was so not a morning person.

"How'd you sleep?" he asked, handing over a fresh mug that smelled out-of-this-world amazing.

"I didn't much," she admitted because there was no point in lying. Her mind had gone round and round last night on the possibility of being a Butler. What if she was? What if she wasn't? How could any of this be true? Granted, her father hadn't been the warm-and-fuzzy type, but he'd always been there for her and she knew without a doubt that he'd loved her. Right? Was he obstinate? Yes. A slave to routine? Absolutely. A bad person? No way. And yet an annoying little voice inside her head kept reminding her that she'd always felt like he was holding back, keeping her at arm's length.

"You didn't like the bed?" That he seemed concerned about her comfort was as sweet as it was surprising.

"It was great. It's me. I kept going over everything that happened yesterday." She bit back a yawn as she took a seat at the table. In a few minutes the caffeine would kick in and her day could begin. In times like these, she wished she had an IV of the brown liquid.

"I'm assuming you're talking about the incident with the white sedan." He took the seat across from her and she ignored the way his nearness made her pulse sprint.

"That and so much more." She made eyes at him before taking another sip.

He didn't seem to know how to react to that and she certainly didn't.

"Did you remember anything else from the events of yesterday?"

"Just what you already know." She shook her head. "I keep going in circles. The white sedan was scary. Being told Mike Butler might be my father completely threw me for a loop. And then there's the 'welcome' message on the mirror. Add to all that the drama I've been experiencing with my ex and it feels like my life has spun out of control."

"That would be a lot for anyone to process." He drummed his fingertips on his coffee mug.

"I just keep asking myself, 'Why? Why me? Why now?' It feels a little like the walls are caving in." She couldn't look directly at him when she spoke. Guilt, or maybe it was embarrassment, assaulted her.

"Bad things happen to good people every day." There was something in his voice she couldn't put her finger on.

How many times in the past few weeks had

she tried to convince herself that was true? It didn't stop the black cloud from hanging over her head ever since this whole ordeal with Owen had begun. "I haven't asked for anything from the Butlers, so why would one of them target me?"

"Not yet. But you could, especially if paternity proves true." He made a good point.

"I wouldn't," she countered.

"They don't know that." Right again.

"Granted, they have no idea who I am, but if Ed Staples is to be believed, they shouldn't know about me at all." It was fact and had gotten lost in the stress of yesterday. "The envelope he gave me was sealed and he said he didn't even know what it contained until he took one look at me."

The cowboy sat there, sipping his coffee, contemplating.

Madelyn needed to get up and move. Her nerves were on edge and she needed to keep busy. Overthinking something never made it better. "I promised you breakfast. I hope you have a working toaster."

His eyes widened. "Based on your reaction last night to the thought of cooking, I thought we could go out for breakfast tacos."

"Good call." Madelyn's smile died on her lips. Her mind kept circling back to her problems and who was trying to get rid of her.

"This doesn't look good for the lawyer," Hudson finally said, bringing the conversation back down to reality. "He's the only one who knew when you were coming, that you were coming at all."

"Yes, but I was with him when the note was written on my mirror," she clarified.

"He could've slipped a few bucks to one of the workers at the Red Rope Inn." Hudson drained his cup and rose to his feet. "Let's go find out who was working besides Kelsey and who might've had access to your room. We'll pick up breakfast on the way."

"I'm pretty sure Kelsey isn't going to speak to me again. She'll most likely hit the panic button if she sees me so much as pull into the parking lot." Madelyn followed suit with the cowboy, welcoming the caffeine boost.

"I'd let you wait in the truck but I'd rather keep you where I can see you." He reminded her of just how much danger she was in.

She couldn't argue with his point.

"And then we can talk to the lawyer," he said. "I'll see what kind of feel I get from him."

"What would Ed Staples have to gain from hurting me, though?" She followed Hudson to the garage, where he opened the passenger door of the truck for her.

"Someone's trying to scare you away, keep you silent, and I'm not ready to rule anyone out just yet." He stepped up to the driver's side in one easy motion, whereas she'd clumsily climbed into the passenger seat. He moved fluidly, with athletic grace.

He also brought up another issue.

"The lawyer summoned me, so why would he try to run me off the road?" she asked. "Wouldn't he just ignore his boss's request? After all, Staples is the one who brought this to my attention in the first place."

"Good point. Although, he might've figured news would get out eventually. Or he could be innocent and someone could be monitoring his calls. I'm assuming he used a cell phone?" He navigated down the path toward the gate, and she couldn't help but think that just yesterday morning she'd been on this same road.

"The call had a cell-quality to it," she admitted. She was used to picking up on things like that in her line of work.

"The Butler estate is worth a fortune. Billions of dollars are on the line. Someone could be monitoring his phone activity." He pulled onto the street and a cold shiver raced down her spine, as she thought about the events that had unfolded the last time she was there.

"I need to get my car." She didn't like the thought of leaving her convertible in the motel parking lot, exposed.

"You can drive it back to the house and park in the garage for safekeeping." He seemed to pick up on the reason for her concern.

"I should find another place to stay. I've already inconvenienced you enough." She pulled out her cell. She could find another hotel using her phone's app.

"At this point, I'd be more comfortable if you stayed with me at the ranch. I'd like to see this through and make sure you're okay. The sheriff's office is too busy to put any manpower on your complaint and it's clear someone doesn't want you here. You could go home and not be safe until this case is resolved." He gripped the steering wheel. "It's your call, but you're welcome to stay at the ranch."

She'd thought that renting a room from a bed-and-breakfast could work but she knew security would be too lax. Then there was a hotel option, which would be expensive. Her budget was tight but she didn't feel right living off the graciousness of a stranger, either. Besides, experience had taught her depending on others was a mistake.

"It's nice of you to offer, but—"

"Think about it, at least," he said. "Hotels aren't the most secure and your car would be exposed. We have no idea who could be behind this."

She thought about what Owen had scrawled across her hood with spray paint. At the very least she didn't want to deal with him finding her and pulling another stunt like that one. A restraining order wasn't exactly an ironclad guarantee that he wouldn't show up. She'd chew on that a little longer and see how she felt after talking to the workers at the Red Rope Inn.

Her cell buzzed in her hand, startling her. And then she stared at the screen, unsure if she should answer.

"Who is it?" Hudson asked.

"Ed Staples."

"Answer it and let him know that he's on speaker." He'd used his cop tone. He had to have been a cop, right?

"This is Madelyn." She couldn't say for sure what Hudson's background was and there hadn't been any clues at his house, either. "I'm with a friend and you should know that he can hear the call."

"Are you all right?" There seemed to be genuine concern in his voice.

"Why wouldn't I be?" She had no plans to tip her hand about the message on the mirror. If he was involved she might be able to trip him up.

"You tore out of here pretty fast yesterday," he stated.

She couldn't argue with that. "Is that the reason you called? To check on me?"

"I'm concerned at how you're taking the news. I can only guess how confusing this must be." He seemed sincere and honest. But after Owen, she didn't exactly trust her instincts about people anymore and especially men. She tried not to chew on the irony of that thought considering she'd just stayed in a strange man's home.

"All I have is a piece of paper claiming that Mike Butler is my father. That doesn't change a thing, in my opinion," she said as coolly as she could.

"Oh." What was in his voice? Shock. Yes. But what else?

Disbelief.

"What's wrong, Mr. Staples? Are you surprised that I'm not jumping all over a claim to

Mike Butler's fortune?" She listened for background noise to figure out his location.

"To be honest? Yes." There was nothing to give away his surroundings. It was quiet and he was most likely calling from that same office inside the Butler camp where they spoke less than twenty-four hours ago.

"Well, then you obviously don't know me very well, do you?" she asked, but it was rhetorical.

He started to say something but she cut him off.

"Guess you had me figured wrong," she said. Was she trying to prove how different she was from a Butler child? Probably. But it didn't stop the little blossom of hope that all this was a bad dream and she'd be getting back to her life—a life without Owen—by tomorrow.

"Not really," he stated, and there was an astonished quality to his voice.

"What's that supposed to mean?" she asked.

Staples hesitated. Then came, "That's exactly what your father would've said."

Chapter Eight

"My father is Charles Kensington until proven otherwise." The slight tremor to Madelyn's voice belied her certainty. She was coming off strong, reassured. Based on Hudson's experience, her house of cards was about to tumble down and she knew it. That was the reason for the tough-guy act.

"Will you be able to stop by today and discuss what this news means?" Ed Staples asked.

"I'll think about it," she said. "I have a few things that I have to take care of first."

"Call me when you're ready and I'll arrange for you to meet the others," he stated.

She hoped he was talking about the Butler kids and not more people like her. How many kids did Maverick Mike have?

"I will."

It took a few seconds of Madelyn staring out the front windshield for her shoulders to relax into the seat after she dropped her phone into her purse.

"How did your father react to the news?" Hudson asked. Years of experience had taught him to recognize when someone was being honest, and Staples had sounded sincere. Hudson wasn't ready to scratch the lawyer's name off his suspect list but he'd moved it to the bottom for the time being.

"I haven't spoken to him yet," she responded.

"Come again?" he asked. That was the first place she should've checked to figure out if Butler was her biological father. A point could be made that the man she believed to be her parent might not have known she wasn't his. But Hudson was jumping the gun.

"He didn't return my call yesterday, okay. It's not like I didn't try." There was so much frustration in her voice that Hudson could tell there was a bigger story. One she didn't seem ready to share. He was smart enough not to poke an angry bear, so he left the subject alone.

They ate in the small breakfast taco shack and then made their way to the Red Rope Inn.

Hudson parked near the lobby's glass doors. "Follow my lead."

"Ask for Trent. He was working when I checked in yesterday," she said.

"What does he look like?" he asked.

"Black hair. Brown eyes. Not too tall, maybe five foot nine. Pretty young, I'd say maybe twenty-three. He had a mole toward the bottom left of his chin. He was reasonably attractive." Her keen observation skills reminded him that he was dealing with a reporter. He needed to keep that thought close when the urge to kiss her tried to overpower common sense again.

A different worker was behind the counter today. He was fairly young, midthirties, and already starting to lose his hair. Hudson made a mental note of his description. Maybe they could get a copy of the schedule.

"Is Trent here?" he asked after taking Madelyn's hand. Frissons of electricity vibrated up his arm. He did his level best to ignore them, especially since the memories of that kiss from yesterday had been on his mind all night.

"He called in sick," the worker said. "I'm Robert. How can I help you?"

A red flag just shot up in Hudson's mind, and based on the way Madelyn's fingers tensed, the same happened to her.

"Is the manager in?" Hudson asked.

"You're looking at him," Robert said with a curious look. "What can I do for you?"

"There was a woman here yesterday by the

name of Kelsey," he continued, wondering why the manager would be behind the counter helping walk-ins. Then again, Red Rope Inn looked like a small operation, so it could be possible.

"Brownish, reddish hair. About yay tall?" Robert held his hand out flat underneath his eyes. He was about five foot ten and was indicating roughly Madelyn's height.

Hudson glanced toward Madelyn, who was nodding.

"Yeah, that's the one," he said. "Does she work today?"

"I'm afraid not and she won't be back." Robert frowned.

"Really?" Madelyn dropped his hand.

"Kelsey turned in her resignation last night," Robert said with a shake of his head. "Said she couldn't handle the job anymore."

"Hard to find dependable help these days," Hudson agreed as more red flags shot up.

"You're telling me," Robert said. "All over

some kind of stink made yesterday from one of our guests."

Hudson could guess who that meant. He reached back for Madelyn's hand, found it and ignored the unwelcome charge of electricity pulsing up his arm from contact once again.

"My girlfriend and I wanted to thank her. She and Trent did a great job when we checked in last night," Hudson lied. Didn't sound like Robert knew what was going on. "I guess there's no way you could give us her address so we could stop by on our way out of town."

Robert's head was already shaking. "Sorry. Can't give out personal information of current or former employees. Corporate would have my head on a platter."

"With all the lawsuits going around, I understand," Hudson said in a move of solidarity. "We can't leave a note for her since she's no longer employed here."

"We get paychecks day after tomorrow. She

didn't tell me to mail hers when she resigned and she's one of the few who still get theirs on paper, so I'm guessing she'll swing by. I could pass along a thank-you note then," Robert offered.

"Any idea what time that might be?" Hudson asked.

Robert seemed to catch on. He shrugged, like he was trying to look casual, but sweat beaded on his forehead. "Not sure."

"We'll do a note, then." Hudson turned to Madelyn. "Do you want to do the honors?"

She nodded and he could almost see the wheels turning behind her eyes. "Is there a pen and paper I can use?"

Robert produced both and then waited while she scribbled.

They thanked him and left quickly. The door had barely closed behind them when she asked, "Doesn't it seem suspicious that Kelsey quit and Trent called in sick?"

"Absolutely," he agreed.

Her phone buzzed and she looked up at him with a mix of fear and anxiety.

"Might want to see who that is," he said.

She did.

"A number I don't recognize but this is the second time they've called. I figured it was… *him*… I didn't answer last night," she said.

"Is there a message?" His brow shot up.

She nodded. "I forgot to listen to it. My mind's been on a million other things."

He could understand why she'd want to shut down last night. She put her phone to her ear and stilled as she listened to the recording. Hudson glanced at her, ignoring the memory of her lips on his from last night—a memory that had pervaded his thoughts and made sleep impossible. He almost laughed out loud at that one. He hadn't slept a straight eight in more than a year.

"What the…?" She paused. "Oh, you've got to be kidding me."

"What is it?" He pulled out of the parking lot.

"That was Kelsey's lawyer. She's suing me for putting her under duress yesterday," she said, indignant.

"I guess news that you're a Butler is out."

"*Might* be a Butler," she corrected, "and who would do something like this anyway?"

"Now I really wish we had Kelsey's address," he said. "Hold on. I think I might know a person who can help us."

Hudson turned the wheel and headed back to the sheriff's office. A few turns and fifteen minutes later he parked in front of Sawmill's office. The buzz of reporters was everywhere and a few rushed over, swarming his truck. One yelled, "No one important!" and the rest scattered back to their vans with disappointed looks.

"This place is a zoo," she said.

"Keep your head down, eyes forward."

"What are we doing here?" Her eyes were wide.

"Pretending to follow up on your complaint from last night." Hudson took Madelyn's hand, ignoring the spark ignited by contact. It struck him that the reporters dismissing them meant her news hadn't really gotten out. What did that say? Only a few people knew…a few insiders, and that made him think the attacks on Madelyn were coming from inside the Butler camp.

"Doris," Hudson said over the hum of activity in the sheriff's office.

She glanced up and her gaze stopped on Madelyn. A look of shock crossed her worn features. The extra activity seemed to be taking a toll on her but she quickly recovered with a smile.

"How's my favorite person in all of Cattle Barge doing this morning?" she asked Hudson.

"You can't be talking about me since I don't live in town," he said, returning her smile.

"Even so, I rarely ever get the pleasure of your company twice in one week. Who's the pretty lady?" She smiled at Madelyn.

He introduced them.

"Nice to meet you," Madelyn said, breaking their link in order to shake Doris's outstretched hand.

"What brings you into town?" Doris asked with a quirked eyebrow.

"My friend is visiting and had an incident on the highway yesterday afternoon." Could he really only have known Madelyn for a day? Being around her felt natural, like they'd known each other for years instead of hours.

Doris rocked her head. "She's the one?"

"Afraid so." Neither seemed ready to say she was also the one from the complaint at the motel last night.

"The sheriff told me about what happened in

our briefing first thing this morning," she said. "Our town is normally a great place to be. I'm sorry your experience doesn't match."

It was good that Sawmill was talking about the incident. Assigning resources was another story and that was where the investigation was falling short. "I know how busy things are around here and a case like hers is likely to be set aside when a murder investigation the scale of Mike Butler's makes news. I thought I might do a little digging on my own. It would be a great help if you could tell me the names of a few employees at Red Rope Inn."

"I can't do that," Doris insisted with a cluck of her tongue.

He'd expected as much.

"There was a girl working last night. Kelsey Shamus," Madelyn continued without missing a beat. "I got a call from her lawyer. She's suing me because she thinks I traumatized her while I was upset about someone gaining access to my room without my permission."

Doris gasped. "What on earth? From what I heard, you were the victim. Why would she…? Never mind… People surprise me all the time. I should know better than to be shocked by anything these days."

"The person who wrote the threat on my mirror had to have had a key. Kelsey told me no one had access," Madelyn continued.

"What about housekeeping?" Doris clucked her tongue again.

"Exactly. That's what I asked. I'd had a hard day and probably came off a little too strong." Madelyn's conspiratorial tact seemed to be working because Doris was getting visibly upset.

"Who wouldn't?" Shoulders stiff, Doris was indignant now.

"I know, right," Madelyn agreed. "Looking

back, I was probably a little too harsh with her but it's not like I cursed her out."

"You had a right to, though," Doris said on a huff.

Madelyn was a damn good journalist. She might not want to admit it, but she'd make one fine lawyer, too.

"A guy named Trent was working when I checked in. Do you know him?" she asked.

"He's the Buford boy," Doris admitted.

And, *bingo*, they had a last name. The fact that Madelyn was a good investigator shouldn't clench his stomach in the way it did. Her curiosity about him would eventually win out and she'd dig around in his background.

"Does he live in town?" Madelyn pressed.

Doris glanced around and then leaned forward. "He rents a house with the Mackey boy over on Pine next door to the CVS, same block."

"Thank you so much, Doris. You've been a huge help," Madelyn said with a satisfied smile.

Hudson took note of the fact that she seemed able to turn her charm on readily in order to get what she wanted. Reporters were bigger chameleons than detectives when they needed to be. He also reminded himself that they didn't have to follow the law and that put them in the same category as criminals in his book.

His back stiffened when Madelyn reached for his hand. He forced a smile, keeping up the charade in front of Doris. The second the two of them left the building he intended to let go.

And that was exactly what he did.

MADELYN HAD JUST scored a major win for the team, so she was caught off guard when Hudson dropped her hand the second they walked into the parking lot.

The drive to Pine Street was quiet and she

was left wondering what had changed between them. Something had. But the handsome cowboy wasn't talking and she didn't have the energy to push. He was helping her and she would leave it at that. Plus, they had a lead and that was progress in one area of her turned-inside-out life.

Pine Street had a row of historic-looking houses. She figured they rented for top dollar given the craze for authentic vintage-home charm with modern redesigns and appliances. Hudson walked a step ahead of her and banged on the door with law-enforcement fervor. Whatever had happened back at the sheriff's office had snapped him into cop mode. Although, he had yet to admit his background to her, which begged the question why.

She shelved those thoughts for now. The familiar tingle of excitement that accompanied a break in a big story tickled her stomach. Her pulse sped up, too, along with an adrenaline spike.

If Trent truly was sick, and no one seemed to believe that line, it stood to reason he'd be home.

No one came to the door and there was no sign of movement in the house. It was quarter after ten in the morning, so Trent could be asleep and his roommate, the Mackey boy Doris had mentioned, might be at work. Didn't normal people mostly have nine-to-five jobs now? Madelyn worked all the time and, as a rancher, so would Hudson. But they were outliers.

Disappointment settled in with the second round of bam-bam-bam. The door rattled.

So close…

And then she heard the creak of pressure on wood floors, a glorious sound. But then nothing.

Hudson pressed his face up to the window and muttered a curse at the same time she did.

"That's him," she said. Trent was trying to run. Her pulse pounded.

"Stay here. I'll cover the back," Hudson said in that authoritative voice reserved mostly for people who wore a badge. She'd been told mothers had that same tone but she'd have to take it on face value given that she'd never known hers.

His heavy footsteps disappeared around the side of the house and all she could hear was him shouting at someone.

Madelyn took off after them, pushing her legs to catch up to the two men running in front of her. Hudson's large frame blocked her view of Trent. Her lungs squeezed as they rounded the corner, reminding her how infrequently she'd used that gym membership she'd bought for herself at Christmas and how little she'd adhered to the New Year's resolution that she'd keep up with the workouts. She pushed through burning thighs as Hudson tackled the guy in front of him.

The two of them were fast, so it took a few beats for her to catch up. By the time she did, Hudson was straddled over the younger man's body.

"It's not him," she said through quick breaths, grasping at the cramp in her right side.

"I told you to stay put," he said, his words angry. He hardly seemed affected by the chase, whereas the young guy underneath him was breathing heavy. There was a small satisfaction in that.

"When you ran, I followed," she said, bending forward and glancing back toward the house.

Hudson made a frustrated sound as he turned his attention to the blond-haired twentysomething guy. "Who are you?"

"Dude, what's your problem?" Blond-hair responded.

"You didn't answer my question." Hudson reared his fist back.

"Hold on a second." Blond-hair winced, readying himself for impact.

"Tell me your name," Hudson shouted.

"Brayden Mackey," he responded, turning his head and squinting.

"Where's Trent?" Hudson's posture tensed even more, his fist a few feet from Brayden's face.

"He's gone, dude. He told me to run out the back door and get as far away as I could while he took off out the front," Brayden said.

They'd been played.

Chapter Nine

A ten-minute conversation with Brayden revealed how little he knew about Trent's activities. Frustration at being so close and the only lead slipping through their fingers nipped at Madelyn as she listened. Apparently, the two had been roommates for the past year. Brayden believed that Trent had switched his days off.

"I don't know what you think he's into but Trent's a good dude," Brayden said.

"I'm sure he is. But in my experience innocent people don't run, Brayden," Hudson said through even breaths. On the other hand, Madelyn was still trying to recover from their late-morning run.

Trent was guilty of something.

Brayden shrugged. "He doesn't *party*, if you know what I mean. That was my biggest requirement for being roommates. I'm not into drugs and wild parties."

"You seem like a straight-up guy. You don't mind if we check out your place, do you?" Hudson asked.

"I've got nothing to hide," Brayden defended.

Hudson hopped to his feet in a smooth motion and offered a hand up to the younger man. Brayden took it and the two of them followed him back to his house. The place looked cleaner than a typical bachelor pad. Just as Madelyn had suspected, walls had been taken down in order to give the ground floor as much of an open concept as the older construction would allow. Brayden seemed to take great pride in the place. The furniture was simple and modern. There was a surprising amount of food in the kitchen for two bachelors. In the living room, a flat-screen TV flanked one wall and a gaming system of some sort was still on.

"We were playing when you knocked." Brayden motioned toward the screen.

"Popular game," Hudson agreed. A man in battle fatigues held out a gun in the center of the screen. There was a map in the top right corner. Madelyn had heard of the game before but she couldn't remember the title. Something about planting bombs and counterterror attacks.

Two empty cups of coffee sat on the coffee table next to a plate with a few crumbs still on it.

"You don't think it's suspicious that someone knocks on the door and then your friend bolts?" Hudson asked, and he was probably trying to ascertain if Brayden's story could hold water.

"Sure, at first. He said that it's no big deal

but he wanted me to run out the back door and distract you. Said he might've forgotten to pay a bill or something and that he'd take care of it later," he said.

"And you believed him?" Hudson asked.

"He's never given me a reason not to trust him until now." Brayden rubbed the scruff on his chin. On close examination, he couldn't be more than twenty-six years old. "Are you like cops or something?"

"You have a nice place," Madelyn said to distract him.

Brayden smiled and she was pretty sure his eyes lit up, too.

Okay, she wasn't flirting but he seemed to take it that way. Hudson stepped in between the two of them, blocking Brayden's line of sight.

"Where's Trent's room?" he asked.

"The bedrooms are upstairs. Follow me." Brayden took the lead. He stopped at the top of the stairs. "I don't feel right letting you in my roommate's private space. I don't even go in there. It's why we get along. We don't mess in each other's personal area."

"Tell him that I gave you no choice. If he's a good guy, like you say he is, there's nothing to hide. We won't find a thing and we'll be out of your hair in ten minutes." Hudson maintained steady eye contact as he spoke, only glancing away when he was finished. He stood tall with his shoulders back, communicating confidence.

"Something you said has been bothering me," Brayden admitted. "Innocent people never run. I've seen that on cop shows and, whatever, just don't mess things up in there. But if you find anything to be concerned about, tell me what it is."

"You have a deal." Hudson offered a handshake.

Brayden took the outstretched hand and then

stepped aside to make room for them on the landing.

There were two bedrooms upstairs and a bathroom they must share. Hudson reached for Madelyn's hand and electricity pinged through her with contact. Neither the time nor the place, she thought. He was only making a show of them being together and it meant nothing to him.

Trent's room was messier than downstairs but not by a whole lot. His wallet was on his dresser along with his keys. Hudson opened it and found the usual: credit cards, license, a few twenties along with a two-dollar bill. A laptop was on his bed and there was a stack of clothes piled next to a hamper. It seemed like every man's room she'd been in, be it friend or more, had that same mound of clothes right next to the hamper. What was up with that?

The covers were mussed on the platform-style bed. There was a fistful of change on the nightstand along with chargers. Hudson had scanned the room as he walked it and now his full attention was on the laptop.

"Do you happen to know his password?" he asked Brayden, who was hovering at the door, looking uncomfortable. Did his pinched expression have anything to do with his suspicion that his roommate might've done something wrong, or was it because he'd just allowed strangers to violate their privacy pact? Brayden seemed like a straight-up guy. She decided it was the latter.

"Can't help you there, dude," he said. "We don't share that kind of information."

Madelyn figured as much.

"What's his birthday?" Madelyn asked, figuring most people's passwords used those numbers.

Brayden shot her an are-you-kidding-me look. "He's smarter than that."

Madelyn had no doubt. It seemed like most

twentysomethings knew ten times as much as she did about technology.

"Most people use a pattern on the keyboard," Hudson said.

"Not likely, but I have no idea and I never ask." Brayden shifted his weight to his right foot.

"Do you have any idea where your buddy might've taken off to?" Hudson asked after three failed attempts to hack Trent's password.

"None at all." He shook his head. "But then, I didn't see any of this coming."

He had a point there. He'd seemed genuinely surprised by the revelations so far.

"What about a girlfriend?" Hudson pushed off the bed and stood. She was reminded again at how intimidating his height could be.

"We don't get into that with each other," Brayden said.

And that seemed odd.

"Surely you'd know if he was serious about

someone," Hudson said. "Wouldn't he bring her home with him?"

Brayden shrugged again. "I guess so. He goes out and there've been a few times when he didn't come home lately." His eyes flashed toward Madelyn. "I figured he met someone. But we don't talk about stuff like that. We don't usually work the same shifts, so when we do cross over we're downstairs gaming."

Sounded about right to Madelyn, given their ages.

"Mind if I ask where you work?" Hudson was taking in the scene, leaning a little toward Brayden, and based on the change in Hudson's body language, she figured he wanted the young guy to feel like he was listening.

"I work in the IT department for the Gaming Depot," he supplied. "Everything you saw downstairs we got for free."

"Nice," Hudson said, and she could see that Brayden was relaxing a little, Hudson was gaining trust inch by inch, and she couldn't help but think that he would've made one heck of a journalist. If he didn't dislike them so much.

"Mind if we head back downstairs?" Brayden asked, stepping aside to let them leave the room and head down the steps. He relaxed a little more once they were in the living room.

"Give Trent a message for us?" With his arms crossed, Hudson's posture was loose and open.

"Sure thing, dude." Brayden swayed slightly, leaning a little closer to Hudson and mirroring his body language. The move was totally on a subconscious level and Madelyn knew that Hudson was gaining ground. She appreciated his skills but the average Joe wouldn't be that good.

"Tell him to give me a call. We just want to ask a few questions. We're not trying to collect on a bill. We just want to clear up what we think might be a misunderstanding. Ask him a few questions." Hudson asked for a pen and paper and scribbled down his cell number. "Have him call when he gets home, okay?"

"I'll pass along the message," Brayden promised.

"Oh, and one more thing. What kind of car does he drive?" Hudson asked, stopping at the door.

"White Jeep. Why?" Brayden asked.

"Just wanted to know in case I pass him in the street. We're not cops. We're not here to arrest your friend or make his life miserable. He doesn't owe us any money. All we want is to ask a few questions." Hudson opened the door and then stopped. "By the way, did he seem sick to you this morning?"

Brayden shot a quizzical look toward Hudson. "Not at all. Why?"

"He's not ill?"

"Seemed fine to me," Brayden said.

"His boss said he called in sick at work today.

You guys share rent on this place?" Hudson continued.

"Yeah."

"Make sure he pays up early. Wouldn't want any late fees," Hudson said as he opened the door and walked out.

Damn fine investigative work, if anyone asked Madelyn. Brayden had doubts about his roommate now. From here on out, he'd notice things. She figured that Hudson had plans to circle back in a few days and ask more questions if Trent didn't call, and there was about a fifty-fifty chance Trent wouldn't, based on her experience.

Next time, Brayden wouldn't let Trent run.

MADELYN CALLED HER father's number three times in a row, needing to hear the sound of his voice as she waited to hear back from Ed Staples. He didn't pick up, which wasn't a huge surprise. She pressed the phone to her ear, listening to his recorded message.

"Everything okay?" Hudson asked, breaking into the moment. He surprised her and she quickly wiped the stray tear from her eye before he could see that she was crying.

"Yes. I'm just a little tired. I didn't sleep as much as I would've liked last night." There was no conviction in those words. She couldn't fake being okay. But as she looked out over his expansive property, a sense of calm washed over her. The place was peaceful. She had to give him that. They'd returned to the ranch so that Hudson could take care of his animals and she hadn't heard him walk up behind her until he was right next to her. He folded his hands and rested his elbows on the top railing of the wood fence.

It was hot outside but Madelyn liked the heat. She angled her face toward the sun and closed her eyes. "Ever get the feeling like you're in a nightmare that won't end and you can't wake yourself up?"

"Every day," he said, and there was so much depth to his voice, like a river that had cut its way through granite to carve out its path.

"Where'd you live before?" she asked.

"It's not important," he mumbled, but it was to her. He was as unobtainable as every important man in her life had been. Was that the appeal? The reason her heart fluttered every time he was near?

Madelyn let the sun warm her skin. "My high school coach called to personally invite me to a ceremony honoring my swimming accomplishments."

"Sounds like a big deal," he said.

"It is. The school's planning a whole thing around a couple of us. We're being inducted into the hall of fame," she said. "I called my father to tell him about it and he didn't pick up.

He hasn't called back. He calls on the first of the month without fail and nothing in between."

Tears surprised her, burning the corners of her eyes.

"He sounds reliable." Hudson was trying to make her feel better.

"That, he is. Unless you consider that he might have been keeping a huge secret from me my entire life." So much about her childhood made sense if she wasn't really a Kensington but a Butler.

"I'm truly sorry about your mother." He paused for a beat. "Did your father remarry?"

"Thank you and no. He's been dating the same woman for as long as I can remember. They never married," she stated. "She cooks for him on Thursdays and he takes her out on Sunday nights. Says Saturday is too busy and it's hard to get a table."

Hudson looked out onto the pasture. She expected him to throw a few words on the wall to see if they'd stick, like the few people she'd opened up to over the years always had. They'd say things like, "I'm sure he loved you." Or, "Men are like that sometimes."

Empty words never made a hard situation better.

The cowboy put his arm around her shoulders and she leaned into him.

"Kids should feel loved every day of their lives. They grow up too fast as it is, especially when they lose someone they love so young." His voice wasn't more than a whisper in her hair and yet there was so much comfort in his words.

"Thank you," she said back to him, matching his cadence.

And then she surprised herself in turning to face him, pushing up to her tiptoes and kissing him. His muscles tensed, his back ramrod straight. She trailed her fingers along the strong muscles in his shoulders and gazed up at him.

His eyes darkened with hunger as his tongue slicked across his bottom lip. Madelyn couldn't help herself. She nipped at the trail and he took in a sharp breath.

"This isn't a good idea," he said, and the mystery surrounding him was most likely half the appeal. She told herself that if they went down that road—the one where they had incredible sex—that would somehow dim the attraction between them. Or maybe she was just searching for comfort, for one night of distraction in this crazy mixed-up world that had become her life. She hadn't truly felt like she belonged in someone's arms in…in… How sad was it that she couldn't remember how long? Maybe never?

And yet being with Hudson on his land brought her dangerously close to just that, a feeling of security.

That hot stove was waiting to burn her, so she took a step back, trying to get a handle on her overwrought emotions. Having her life turned upside down was most likely causing these intense emotions coursing through her, she told herself.

"I know I said going ahead with whatever is happening between us isn't smart but stopping it feels like a decision we'll regret," he said. His voice was low and gravelly, and hinted of great sex.

"Then tell me something about yourself. Something that even Doris wouldn't know. Because I don't want to go there with you, a stranger, without feeling like I know who you are," she said, and her voice came out way more desperate than she wanted to admit. Was this another attempt to heal past relationships? To attain the impossible?

"My mother died when I was barely out of high school. I never knew my father," he said, not breaking eye contact.

It seemed like they had more in common than

either of them realized. In so many ways Madelyn didn't feel a connection to hers. What did she know about Charles Kensington other than surface stuff, like the fact he watched football every Sunday while eating Andy Capp's Hot Fries with a Bud Light chaser.

"I don't even know my father's favorite color. I lived with the man for eighteen years of my life and I have no idea what his favorite flower is. It's like we lived side by side in tandem, but not in sync." She flashed her eyes at him, fighting back the swell of tears threatening. Emotions were taking over and embarrassment heated her cheeks for being so point-blank with a near-stranger. Only Hudson didn't feel like a stranger. "Obviously, I overthink things."

"It's not too much to ask to know little things about the person who is supposed to love you the most," he said, adding, "My favorite color is powder blue, like the early-morning sky in spring and your eyes."

A trill of awareness skittered across her skin.

They both stood there for several seconds and she was certain he was feeling the same thing. She could practically touch the current running between them, lighting her senses and tugging her toward the strong man standing in front of her. She may not know who he really was but her body didn't seem to care.

"Did he talk about your mother growing up?" he asked, his serious eyes intent on her.

"Hardly ever," she said. "He let me keep a picture of her next to my bed, and I talked to it all the time when I was little, like she'd somehow magically appear."

His smile was like stepping into a cool natural spring and out of the heat when the sun started to scorch her skin.

"I'm not trying to make you uncomfortable and force you into talking about whatever you've been through that makes you prefer the company of animals to people. All of this has me wondering if I can really ever trust anyone. Do I really know anything about my past? Or was it all a lie? I'm questioning everything now," she said. It struck her as odd that she might not really know the most basic thing about herself, who her father was.

"What about DNA testing?" he asked.

"I asked Ed Staples about it and he apologized, stating that Mike Butler was cremated. There's no way to get a test now," she said. "I asked about siblings but he doubted anyone would volunteer, although, he agreed to ask. Which leaves me no choice but to go to the judge and ask for a court order."

"And that takes time," he said.

"Money, too," she added. "With the Butler fortune at their disposal, the siblings could tie things up in court for years."

"Leaving you right where you started, with no answers," he stated, turning toward the pasture and clasping his hands again. "We could come at this from a different angle. Why would Mike Butler lie about you being his child?"

"I can't think of one reason. He has nothing to gain and my presence brings shame to his children. I checked online last night and I'm around the same age as his eldest daughter. We both know what that means," she said.

"He was cheating on his wife with your mother."

She turned and gripped the railing. "It also means that both of my parents are dead and I call a stranger 'Dad.'"

Chapter Ten

Dinner came and went, and Madelyn decided it was time to clue her boss in since she might not be returning to work for a while. Harlan picked up on the first ring while she was still debating how much she should share.

"What's the story at the Butler farm?" he immediately asked, a sense of anticipation coming through in his tone. She recognized it immediately because she'd felt it a pair of days ago.

"Ranch," she corrected, and she was mostly stalling for time. He knew the difference and was most likely trying to be funny.

"Is it big or a waste of time?" He skipped right over her comment.

"Turns out, I'm the focus," she said with as even a voice as she could muster.

"A story with Maverick Mike Butler starring you?" he questioned. "I'm not sure that I follow."

"He says I'm his long-lost daughter." The words sounded distant as she spoke them.

"Hold on a damn minute. Are you telling me that you're heir to one of the biggest fortunes in the South—no, check that, in the United States—and you just found out?" Harlan said with more than a hint of admiration.

"It would seem so," she admitted without much enthusiasm.

"And this upsets you *because*?"

"I haven't checked it out yet. Maybe I don't want to get my hopes up," she lied. The truth was that she wished for the life she believed was true before. Even though she and her dad didn't have a perfect relationship, she'd always known that he'd loved her in his own way. Her life made sense to her and was all she'd ever known. There was simplicity in that. Stability. Now the earth had tilted, shifting underneath her feet and throwing everything off balance.

"So how did your mom know Mike Butler?" he asked.

"Good question." She knew more about her so-called father than she did about her own mother, and this revelation put even more distance between her and the truth. In fact, Madelyn had been so wrapped up in everything, she hadn't gotten in touch with the rage she felt at Mike Butler. What little she did know about her mother was that she'd died while giving Madelyn life. That fact had always burdened Madelyn because she'd felt like her mother's death had been her fault. Her mother had died because, being young and broke, there was no insurance. She couldn't afford to give birth in the good hospital in town. She'd had to go to the county hospital where the machines weren't reliable, nurses were overburdened and she'd bled out.

If Madelyn could believe the story she'd been told, her mother had forced Charles to follow the baby because she didn't trust the nurses. Meanwhile, she'd hemorrhaged and it had been too late by the time Madelyn's father had returned to check on her. Madelyn had always believed that her father had blamed himself... but now? She had to wonder if he blamed her instead.

If she stuck around town and found the truth, could she learn more about the mother she'd always wanted?

"Needless to say, I need time off in order to figure this whole crazy ordeal out," she said.

"Keep reports coming and I'll continue your salary," he stated. He wasn't a bad guy so much as a persistent journalist. This news would be huge if it panned out.

"I'll think about it but what I told you is between us for now." She had to consider whether she wanted her life splashed across all the papers. Which was a good point, actually. Had the news leaked? Someone inside the Butler camp had to know, right? "Give me your word you'll keep this quiet until I say."

His hesitation didn't exactly make her feel warm and fuzzy.

"File a story. It can be about anything you want. Just give me something decent to put into print. And, yes, you know that I would never go behind your back." His tone was softer, the human side of Harlan peeking through the hardened reporter who'd seen pretty much everything in his two decades on the job.

"Okay, Captain." He'd said that he didn't like her calling him that and she knew down deep that he'd been kidding. He loved the attention.

Wow, she knew her boss better than her own father. What did that say about her relationship with Charles Kensington?

"Madelyn," he said quietly, as though suddenly realizing the implication. "You want me to do a little digging on the family? They have a lot going on over there in Cattle Barge and I'm not sure I like you being there given the news you just shared."

"I share your concerns. I'll be careful." She decided this wouldn't be a good time to fill him in on what had happened to her since arriving in Cattle Barge, noting the rare fatherly side of Harlan coming through. He was divorced with three children, and by his own admission he'd been too busy chasing stories to watch them grow up. He also said that he had divorce papers documenting how he'd failed his wife, too. Relationships always came with a hefty price tag.

"That jerk leaving you alone, at least?" he

asked, and her heart stuttered. And then it quickly dawned on her who he was talking about.

"Owen's been quiet," she admitted. Thankfully.

"Make sure and lock your doors," he warned, his fatherly instincts ever present. He might not have been there for his own kids but he seemed to be making up for it with his reporters. She thought about how little people really knew about each other. She'd worked for Harlan three years and only knew him on paper. Divorced, father of three, boss. Strange when she thought about how many hours she and her high school friends used to spend getting to know every detail of each other's preferences from favorite ice-cream flavor to whether one would pick quitting school over getting to be a rock star.

"I will. Can you dig around into the background of Hudson Dale? He owns a ranch on the outskirts of Cattle Barge and I'm pretty certain he used to work in law enforcement," she said, a feeling of shame washing over her. She should wait until he was ready to talk but had half convinced herself that she deserved to know given that she was staying in his house. She knew the cop-out immediately. "Actually, hold off on that research for a minute."

"You sure about that?" Even though they were in the same state, he sounded a million miles away.

"Yes. Definitely." Was she? She was sleeping in the house of a man she barely knew, but then, based on recent revelations, how well did she know anyone? "Harlan, what's your favorite color?"

"What?" The query was out of the blue and his reaction said she'd caught him off guard.

"Just curious." She found it odd that she knew so little about the man she worked for and yet trusted implicitly. She knew him about as well as Brayden knew his roommate, Trent, and the two lived under the same roof.

"Orange, I guess. Why the sudden interest?" he asked.

"No reason." She paused a beat. "But thanks for telling me."

A soft knock at the door had her ending the call.

"Dinner's ready," Hudson said, and the familiar sound of his voice settled her taut nerves.

"With everything going on today, we forgot to pick up my car," she said after opening the door.

"We can go after we eat," he said as she passed him.

Another fantastic meal courtesy of Hudson Dale and she had no idea how or where he'd picked up his culinary skills. Curiosity was getting the best of her. She wanted—no, *needed*—to know more about him even though she kept her questions at bay on the ride into town.

One look at her car as he pulled beside it and she gasped. The driver's-side window had a hole in it the size of a brick. And that was exactly what had been flung, she realized as she jumped out of the cab of Hudson's truck. Her presence in town might not exactly be welcome, but damaging her property was a whole other issue. Her thoughts shifted to Owen for a split second. Could he have tracked her down?

No. She'd been careful to make sure that only Harlan knew where she'd gone. And she trusted her boss with her life. Literally, countless times, and he'd come through. A little voice reminded her that if she didn't know her own father she couldn't know anyone else, not even her boss. She shushed it and figured half the reason she was sticking around was to find out more about her mother. More lies. They were mounting. Because she needed to know the truth about so many things in her life.

Mike Butler obviously knew about her. Was

he even sad when he learned that her mother had died? Relieved? Did he get her pregnant and back out of a relationship, not wanting to take responsibility for Madelyn? Had he sat idly by while she and Charles struggled financially? His legitimate kids growing up with every advantage at their disposal? Money. Education. Respect. If he'd offered to pay for medical expenses, and he'd had plenty of money to cover them, would her mother still be alive?

Anger raged inside her.

"Someone's obviously been here," Hudson said, studying her.

Her hands were fisted at her sides. Frustration nipped at her and she wanted to scream. "It's shocking how little people value others' hard work. I mean, I had to save a long time to come up with the down payment and this is the second time it's been vandalized."

She glanced over in time to see his dark brow shoot up. He deserved to know what he was getting into, so she told him about Owen, the threats and the horrible word he'd scribbled across her car's hood.

"I can certainly see you've had a rough go lately," he said sympathetically. "Is your ex the reason you don't trust people?"

His comment scored a direct hit and she wondered what in his past made him the same way. Of course, every time she tried to get him to discuss anything about himself, he shut her down or changed the subject. It was such an odd feeling, too. Because she barely knew him, he'd scarcely told her two things about him, and yet she felt so at ease with him. "He's one in a long line."

Electricity hummed and sensual shivers raced up her arms every time they touched but that didn't throw her off, either. It felt… natural. Which pretty much proved the mind could trick itself into believing anything it yearned for. Like her belief that her mother had been a decent woman. Seriously, what kind of person cheated on her longtime boyfriend, got pregnant and then came back to let him help bring up the child?

Okay, dying couldn't have been part of the plan, so Madelyn could give her mother a break on that count even if there was a bit of residual anger still there. It hadn't exactly been her mother's choice to leave her, but all these revelations explained so much about why her "father" had never been attached to her emotionally. He'd been in love with her mother, had married her and stayed beside her even with a bastard child. And then the woman had gone and died on him, leaving him to bring up… *what?*…the constant reminder of her infidelity.

Was Madelyn being too hard on her mother? On the man she knew as her father? *On herself?* a little voice asked.

"Can you handle driving a pickup?" Hudson broke through her heavy thoughts.

"Yeah." She just stared into the night, the wind knocked out of her. It was only a car window, she reminded herself, something that could be replaced. Why did it feel like someone had shattered her soul?

The internal scars racking up wouldn't be so easy to fix.

"Good, because I want you to take my vehicle home and I'll drive yours," he said.

She turned to him. "Can I ask you something?"

"Fire away."

"Why are you helping me? I mean, you don't have to. No one seems to want me around and that can't be good for your social life once I'm gone. Besides, you don't even know me. I'm a total stranger," she said, the words rushing out.

"This will most likely sound strange, it does even to me, but in some ways, I do feel like I know you," he said with a slight shrug.

"What? Like kindred spirits?" she asked, because she felt the same way even though she was too worked up to admit it right now.

"Something like that. You have a familiar lost look," he said.

"I don't need your pity," she shot back, more affected by those words than if she'd been struck.

"It's more of a kinship. I had that same expression when I came back a year ago," he admitted.

"Did buying a ranch chase away your demons?" she pressed, needing to know more. Heck, anything about the man who'd been her link to sanity.

"Not as much as I'd hoped," he said honestly.

"I should pack up, go home and forget all of this happened. Ever since I arrived in Cattle Barge things have only gotten worse."

"Being on my land, taking care of my animals, is a good distraction. Makes me feel like I'm doing something good," he said with such sincerity there was no way he was lying. "But the nightmares still wake me up. No matter where I go, they follow. And yours will, too."

"Then what do you suggest because I feel like I'm running out of options here," she blurted out on a frustrated sigh.

"Stick around. Follow this thing through. Based on what you said earlier about your ex, going home won't give you a break." He paused a few beats. "Besides, there's a way to find out what the Butlers are thinking."

She caught on to where he was headed with this and she wasn't sure she liked it. "I'm the last person they'll want to see."

"You need to talk to them face-to-face. I'll be there and we can put our heads together after and see what we come up with."

She suddenly felt embarrassed. Talk about unwanted—the Butler children certainly wouldn't welcome their father's illegitimate child with open arms and she wasn't sure how much more rejection she could take. "I don't know."

"The best way to conquer an enemy is to look him in the eye." Hudson was right; she knew that. It was also harder than she imagined.

"What makes you so good at investigating crimes?"

Hudson didn't answer. He asked for her keys and told her that his were still in the ignition.

She took the driver's seat and then rolled the window down on the passenger side as he cleared it. "So, we get to talk endlessly about my life but I still don't get to know anything about yours?"

"I'm the one helping you, and knowing the details of yours might just break this case open," he stated, and she could tell that a wall had come up between them.

"Well, then I'm going home in the morning," she said.

"Suit yourself but that'll hurt you a helluva lot more than it will me." Was that true?

Examining his expression, she decided that it was. And that was exactly why she needed to go.

THE DRIVE HOME alone in her car was too quiet, Hudson thought as he contemplated what Madelyn had said. She'd be crazy to leave now and she didn't strike him as such. There was too much at stake here and they still hadn't tracked down Trent or Kelsey.

Hudson missed the sound of Madelyn's voice but it was dangerous to admit it to himself. He couldn't allow himself to care about her more than he already did. He didn't *care*, he corrected. His law-enforcement instincts had kicked in and he missed the job, the excitement.

Being on a horse ranch, on his land, was good for him. Right?

Rather than go round and round about his

career choice again, he focused on Madelyn. It would be easy enough to schedule a service to swing by and replace the window. Helping her, feeling useful to someone else, was nice. That was what she provided, a welcome reprieve from the doldrums of routine. His life had become too monotonous and the sexy curve of her hips offered a different kind of distraction. He'd dated since returning to Cattle Barge but he was restless. There was a shortage of interesting women and he told himself that Houston had offered more variety and that was why he'd gotten bored here. He'd been going through the motions. But then, didn't that wrap up his life in general?

His personal motivation had waned and he'd thought about selling the ranch, moving Bullseye to a place closer to the city and settling in Dallas or Austin. A change might do him some good. The only thing stopping him was the thought of not spending 24/7 with his horse. He could admit the land held a pull that the city could never have. Moving to Cattle Barge had been meant to stop the nightmares. It hadn't. He still heard Misty scream as the bullet pierced her barely pregnant belly.

As partners, they'd been keeping their relationship a secret from their supervising officer. To say the pregnancy had been a shock was a lot like showing up to a bullfight only to find an empty ice rink. Hudson hadn't been ready to become a father. The guilt for that would haunt him the rest of his life. Not that it mattered. He'd convinced himself that he loved Misty and had stepped up to ask the big question.

She'd said yes.

The rest was history.

At some point, he thought he'd be ready—excited, even—for the marriage. He'd adjusted to the idea of being a father faster than he'd expected. Love for a child could be so instant and required no work on his part.

He and Misty would've made a good family for the child's sake. They got along and shared the same sense of humor. He'd figured it would be a good foundation. She'd been waiting for her transfer to come through so they could make the big announcement and then get married. He'd been the one to suggest holding off until they'd secured their jobs. Dating co-workers was frowned upon by the department, so the news of a pregnancy and quickie marriage would have hurt both of their careers.

That was what he'd been thinking about and not the fact that Misty had said a million times that she didn't want to be pregnant and unmarried. That her mother had done the same and she'd feared having her mother's hard life and bad choices. Every day as a child, Misty had been told how much of an inconvenience she'd been to her mother. Physical bruises could heal and there'd been a few of those. But words left the biggest marks—marks on the heart.

Hudson had let Misty down, too. And he had the nightmares to prove it.

The bullet that had been intended for him had killed two people with one shot.

And he'd lived with the guilt ever since.

Chapter Eleven

"I know your mind is made up and I respect that but leaving now would be a mistake you'll regret," Hudson said as soon as Madelyn stepped out and closed the door to his truck. They'd made it home in record time and he'd been lost in his thoughts about Misty.

"What do you care about my choices?" she shot back as she spun around to walk toward the front door.

He shouldn't want a reporter to stay with him. Her questions were already mounting and she'd need answers soon. If she dug around in his background, she could kick up a whole storm that he wasn't ready to talk about. His chief had taken pity on him when he'd come clean about the pregnancy and relationship, keeping his name out of the papers. If anyone really wanted to snoop around, a connection could be easily made.

Hudson caught Madelyn's arm to stop her from walking away. She needed to hear what he had to say. Then if she decided to leave, so be it. He would've done his part and his conscience would be clear. He almost laughed out loud at that one. If Madelyn left he was sure he'd get even less sleep than he did now.

"I do care that you seem determined to get yourself hurt or killed." Madelyn and Misty couldn't have been more different. There was more of a comradery between him and Misty than the frissons of heat between him and Madelyn. He and Misty had been coworkers with enough sexual chemistry to make going to bed enjoyable. Had there been sizzle? Spark? Not really. His relationship with Misty had been comfortable. She was funny, hot and had kept an emotional distance. Could there have been more between them? Maybe. He figured that no one could get close enough to her to develop real feelings. And that had shocked him even more when she'd become pregnant, because she was on birth control. At least, that was what she'd said.

Sure, they'd spent time together and they'd made love. But their interludes had had more to do with the fact that they worked the night shift when everyone else slept, and had the same time off.

And then she'd admitted to seeing another guy when she thought things might be getting too intense.

Their relationship had developed out of convenience more so than can't-live-without feelings. He cared about her deeply. Misty had been the last person he'd seriously dated and even that had been more like a friends-with-benefits fling. The fact that his feelings didn't run deeper than friendship didn't stop the pain when she'd been killed; losing her and the baby had left a huge gaping hole in his chest. The only way he knew how to close it was to shut down. And that was exactly what he'd done. Quit his job. Moved to Cattle Barge. Shut himself off to the world.

Madelyn stood there, staring at him with a questioning look on her face. He'd slipped into the past and she seemed to know he'd mentally disappeared.

Her foot tapped impatiently and he had the sudden urge to haul her against his chest and kiss her until they both forgot what day it was. And everything else, for that matter. If doing so would solve anything, he'd go all in. But it wouldn't erase the real problems they faced.

This seemed a good time to say, "You can't leave until you know what's going on. You owe yourself that much. This will follow you wherever you go. Talk to the Butlers with me tomorrow and if it doesn't help you can pack up afterward and head back to Houston. No harm. No foul. But leave without that conversation and you're always going to wonder."

Her arms folded across her chest and she sighed sharply, her "tell" that he was making headway.

"What do you have to lose? Your car window needs fixing. I know a guy who can get that done in the morning while we visit the ranch," he added. Hudson wasn't sure why it was so important to him to follow this through with her. But it was. A little voice inside his head said that he didn't want her to leave. That losing her brought back feelings he'd buried a long time ago even before Misty had died. But that didn't make sense. He'd convinced himself that he was immune, his emotions had died with Misty and he didn't want to consider other possibilities, like he'd stuffed his true feelings down deep so that he could do the right thing and marry her in the first place.

Dammit. No. He'd cared for Misty. He'd loved his child.

"I'll call Ed Staples and see if I can arrange it as long as you come with me," Madelyn said, and he was grateful for the distraction. Rehashing the past wouldn't change a damn thing. Hudson should know. He'd done that hundreds of times in the past year.

"I'll put on a pot of coffee," he said.

"Save mine for the morning." She looked at him with the saddest eyes as she held up her phone. "I need to make a call and then I'm going to take a shower and go to bed."

She walked away, waiting for him to unlock the door, and that was probably for the best because his damn arms wanted to hold her. He let them both in, locked the door behind them and moved into the kitchen, where he went to work, making coffee and thinking about the questions she should ask the Butlers.

Shower water kicked on in the other room.

He forced his thoughts away from her naked silky skin in his shower. His grip tightened around the mug as he tried to quell the rising tide of hunger welling inside him.

When he heard the water turn off, he stalked toward the bedroom.

"WISH YOU'D ANSWER my calls. I miss you, Madelyn," the message from Owen began. "I also realize what a jerk I've been. I was hurt and I'm not using that as an excuse but that has to be a little charming, right?"

"It's right up there with being burned at the stake," Madelyn mumbled as she listened to the rest.

"If you'll give me one more chance to prove that I'm not...*that* guy, I promise you won't regret it. We had fun together, didn't we?

There's no reason for it to stop because I got out of hand."

"You really know how to pour it on thick," Madelyn said to the phone as she deleted the message.

A knock at the door startled her.

"Hold on a sec," she said quickly, popping to her feet and glancing down to make sure her towel covered everything. "Okay, come in."

The door opened but Hudson didn't enter. "What did the lawyer say?"

Just the sight of him standing at the door, his strong arms resting against the jamb, brought all kinds of sensual shivers skittering across her sensitized skin. She was very aware of how naked she was underneath that towel as heat rushed through her, settling between her thighs.

"He's setting up lunch for tomorrow." Although she shouldn't compare the two, it was impossible not to notice the differences between

Owen and Hudson. Owen could be charming but his frame was half that of Hudson. Her host was strong and athletic. He didn't give away much but there was something brooding deep inside him and she wanted to know what it was. Owen talked too easily, too much about things that didn't matter.

She tried to convince herself that her finely honed reporter instincts and professional curiosity had her wanting to know more about the handsome cowboy, but there was so much more to it than that.

"Good. Think about what I said earlier." There was something else on his mind but he didn't seem able or willing to find the right words to say it.

"No matter how long I stay here, I want you to know how much I appreciate everything you've done so far," she said, needing to say the words. "I doubt I'd be alive right now if not for you."

"You would. You're smart and beautiful." He started to turn but stopped. "I'd like you to stay, Madelyn."

Her name sounded sweet rolling off his tongue and her stomach flipped hearing his words.

"Because I do care about what happens to you, Madelyn. More than I should."

"HAVE YOU HEARD anything else from Kelsey's attorney?" Hudson asked the next morning. His jeans were low on his hips and he wasn't wearing a shirt. Madelyn shouldn't notice the ripples of muscles cascading from his chest toward that small patch of hair above his zipper.

"Not yet," she admitted, seeking coffee like a missile homes in on its target. She checked out the window on her way to the kitchen and saw that the glass had been fixed. She thanked Hudson for taking care of it. "I thought we could swing by the motel this morning and check on Trent."

The cowboy issued a rare smile. His cheeks dimpled and she decided she liked his face even more.

Two cups of coffee later, they were on the road.

"We played the part of being two people moving through town the other day with the manager. He'll be suspicious if we walk inside the lobby again and he's there," Hudson said as he pulled into the lot of the Red Rope Inn.

"True." Madelyn glanced around and saw a housekeeping cart. "Let's ask."

She hopped out of the pickup and made a beeline toward the cart, which was positioned in front of an open door. "Excuse me."

An older woman wearing a blue pantsuit stepped out. She glanced at her cart like she was waiting for Madelyn to ask for more towels.

"I'm sorry to bother you, but can you tell me if Trent's working the front desk today?"

The woman's head shook. "He's sick."

"Thank you." Madelyn walked back to the truck and closed the door behind her. "He's got quite an illness."

"Interesting," Hudson said. "Kelsey's suing you and Trent has caught one helluva virus. Seems like these two know more than they're telling."

"I checked the news last night and no one's reporting the story about me being a Butler," Madelyn said.

"Now all we have to figure out is who knows," he said, pulling onto the highway.

Forty minutes later, he was being waved through the gates at Hereford.

He parked and followed her to the front door. Madelyn knocked.

"Come in," the woman who'd introduced herself as Ella Butler said from the other side of the door. She hesitated for a long moment before opening it.

"I'm here to see Ed Staples," Madelyn said. Ella looked exactly like her pictures from the society-page stories. Madelyn didn't want to like the woman who was cold-shouldering her, but she did. Even though she'd grown up in the top 1 percent, Ella spent countless hours invested in community projects and volunteer work. She'd been heavily involved in trying to open a new animal shelter, which had put her in the sights of someone determined to stop her because he wanted to buy the land. He'd come close to shooting her to ensure he got it.

Madelyn had combed the internet last night researching each member of the Butler family. She wanted some idea of what she was getting into today. There were four kids—that everyone knew of—two girls and two boys. All had grown into productive, motivated adults, by all accounts, despite having had everything handed to them.

"The family wants to meet you. My sister, Cadence, is recovering from the flu. She thought she could handle all the media attention, so she came home, but it turned out to be too much for her. She caught the first flight out this morning." Something moved behind Ella's gaze that had Madelyn wondering if that were true. A thought struck. Was the media attention getting to the family or was everyone worried now that the Butlers were being singled out and targeted?

Madelyn had read about what happened to Ella. She'd been attacked on a remote piece of the ranch while hiking and had been left for dead. Fortunately, a man on the run had been around to help her recover. A second ambush-style attack had almost killed her but she'd hidden in someone's front landscaping. The details of how she'd survived were unclear except that she'd gone into hiding with the man who'd saved her life and the two had fallen in love. Madelyn introduced Hudson. Ella was courteous but reserved as she greeted him.

Being in Maverick Mike's house was unnerving enough thanks to the tension radiating off Ella. But then, Madelyn hadn't exactly expected the woman to embrace her and call her sister. Heck, Madelyn had been an only child her entire life, so the thought of having siblings didn't exactly bring warm and fuzzy feelings to her, either. Besides, she wasn't there for a reunion. She was there to find the truth.

Slipping into her role as reporter and distancing herself from her own emotions was second nature. She'd done it hundreds of times before, figuring it was so much easier to play a part than to admit to her real feelings of disappointment with family. Damn. That was a little too real for Madelyn.

"Your sister was smart to leave. They won't stop anytime soon." She referred to the vans lining the street.

"Those people out there are like vultures. They'll pick the meat off a carcass and fight each other for the last scrap," Ella said with disdain. "Between them and the people claiming to be a Butler, this town has lost its mind."

Hudson stepped in between her and Ella. "There's no reason to be insulting. Your father summoned her. She had no idea about her heritage before then. And she sure as hell didn't ask to be part of any of you."

He was being defensive and Madelyn shouldn't like that he'd come to her defense as much as she did. Someone sticking up for her was a nice change.

Ella seemed poised to make a comeback.

"It's okay, Hudson," Madelyn interrupted, managing a weak smile as she put a hand on his arm. "I'm sure she wasn't talking about me."

She could handle Ella Butler. From everything she'd heard in the news, Ella was decent and kind. She'd come around to have a civilized conversation at some point.

"Is Mr. Staples here?" Madelyn asked.

Ella seemed to size her up. "I'll get him."

Before she could turn around, footsteps sounded behind her on the tile.

"Thanks for coming," Ed said from the office door. "I apologize for being late. I was held up." His cell was flat on his palm and he shot a look at it. "Crazy thing never stops going off. Please, come in."

Ella unceremoniously turned and walked down the hall without saying another word.

"The boys are waiting in the dining room," Ed said.

She introduced him to Hudson before the three of them made the same trek Ella had moments earlier.

The dining room was beautifully appointed. A long table was the focal point of the room. It looked hand-carved and rustic. Places had been carefully set for six people. But there was not a Butler in sight and she had no idea where Ella had disappeared to.

"I can see that no one wants me here, so this is pointless," Madelyn said, ready to retrace her steps and get far away from the Butler ranch. Being inside made the hairs on her arms prickle. She didn't fit in here and it was obvious. Plus, the whole place set her nerves on edge.

"Give them a chance," Hudson defended, surprising her. "I'm only saying that this has to be as much of a shock to them as it is to you."

"Stay. Please. I'll round everyone up," Ed said. He seemed like the only one trying to build a bridge between them on the Butler side. At least she had Hudson and she'd be lost without him right now.

"Let's sit down and give him a minute to corral the family." Hudson pulled out a chair for her with a wide smile—the smile that was so good at causing her pulse to race and the sensation of birds to flap wildly in her chest.

"Might as well as long as I'm here," she said, returning his smile and hoping she had the same effect on him. One step toward the chair had her rethinking her plan. "On second thought, I might handle them better on my feet."

"Suit yourself." He took a seat next to the one he'd pulled out for her and picked up the glass of lemonade on the place mat.

"That any good?" Her journalism background had her standing behind the chair closest to the exit. It was the trick every journalist knew. Sit closest to the door in order to be the first one out if all hell broke loose. The habit she'd picked up in college had stuck.

"It would taste a hell of a lot better if it was coffee," he stated with a smirk.

Madelyn laughed. She couldn't help herself. Yes, her body was strung tight with so much tension it felt like her muscles might snap. And that was partly why she laughed again.

The click of Ella's heeled sandals cut into the lighthearted moment. Madelyn stiffened as she crossed her arms, steeling herself.

"I apologize for being rude before," Ella started, indicating a seat for Madelyn. The tension in her face hadn't eased in the slightest but her eyes communicated a hint of warmth. "This *situation* is a lot to grasp and seeing you made it all so real. I thought I was better prepared and I realize none of this is your fault."

"For both of us." Madelyn had performed the calculation last night and realized that she and Ella were the same age. Had Madelyn's mother known she was having an affair with a married man? "If it makes you feel any better, I don't want any of your money."

"That wasn't really on my mind." The stress cracks on Ella's forehead said she was being honest. If she was worried about money, it didn't show. "Will we have a chance to meet your mother?"

"She died having me, so that would be impossible," Madelyn stated matter-of-factly. "And, no, I'm not proud of the affair she might've had with your dad."

"I'm sorry for your loss," Ella offered with a look of sympathy. It was too soon to judge her sincerity, but on face value she seemed honest. And then something changed, a split-second reaction.

"Wait a minute. You're not claiming to be a Butler?"

Chapter Twelve

"I don't want to spoil your superior feeling but, no, I'm not," Madelyn stated a little too indignantly. Wearing her emotions on her sleeve was her personal downfall. Professionally, she could hold the line with the best of them. When it came to her personal life she wasn't so skilled at hiding her true feelings.

Ella shot a look at Ed Staples and he returned an I-told-you-so expression.

Two men walked into the room, their boots shuffling on the tiles. They looked almost identical. Tall, probably six feet four inches if she had to guess, and what most would describe as incredibly good-looking, with sandy-blond hair and blue eyes. Madelyn didn't feel a stir of attraction for either one even though she appreciated their good looks. Was it the possibility that they could be related? Did she somehow know they were related?

The first one introduced himself as Dalton and the second as Dade. They were polite, if cautious, as both studied her features. She figured they were looking for any signs of family resemblance. She was, too. And she saw the evidence plainly. All of their hair color was similar and they each had different versions of the same nose. The men had a masculine version, slightly more pronounced. But it was the same nose. A picture on the wall, of Mike Butler surrounded by his children, confirmed they'd gotten the nose from him.

Madelyn absently fingered the dragonfly around her neck with her right hand. Her left searched under the table for Hudson's. She pushed aside the relief she felt when their hands linked, deciding he was the only thing familiar to her in a room full of strangers. Family? It was an odd notion at best.

"I'll just get the sandwiches. I'm sure everyone's hungry and we have quite a bit to discuss after we eat," Ella said, but there was something different about her posture now and Madelyn assumed that it had to do with her revelation.

"I can help," Madelyn offered, standing.

"Oh, okay," Ella said, apparently caught off guard. She was probably used to being in charge and doing things on her own terms, Madelyn guessed.

Madelyn followed her into the expansive kitchen. The place had an old-world-farm-house vibe, with an oversize single sink, white cabinets and granite countertops. There was a wooden table in the kitchen that looked hand-carved and stretched almost end to end. One side of the massive table looked like it was used for food prep and the rest for eating, with bar stools tucked underneath. Platters loaded with finger sandwiches and fresh fruit were set out on top.

"I think we got off on the wrong foot earlier," Ella said as she picked up a tray. "You want to take that one?"

"Sure." Madelyn had whiplash from the change in her demeanor. "Why are you suddenly being so nice?"

"Ed's an old friend of my father's. He's part of a different generation. One that doesn't talk much. He didn't tell me the whole story about you, and I was concerned about your intentions before I realized you don't seem to want this any more than we do." Ella flashed her eyes. "I didn't mean anything personal by that. You seem really nice. Since my father died, we've had people coming out of the woodwork claiming to be one of us, and you seem offended by the idea."

"And that's what you think I am. Basically, a termite coming to eat your house from the inside out," Madelyn stated a little coolly.

"I didn't know what you were. You look like one of us. That's obvious. But the expression on your face before and what you said…you don't want it to be true any more than we do."

"So you win the big prize. You're right. What next?" Madelyn felt a sting from the zinger.

"You're twisting my words, taking them the wrong way," Ella said, balancing the tray on her shoulder. "I just realized that this is as hard on you as it is on us. That's all. And I can sympathize. Don't confuse that for me welcoming you into the family with open arms."

Madelyn took a minute to think about what Ella was saying rather than react.

"I can see your side of the story and how much your life has been turned upside down. I couldn't see beyond my own nose before when Ed said he had a surprise announcement. The news caught us all off guard. I mean, Dad was no saint, but cheating on our mother? I guess I always blamed my mother for abandoning us, disappearing without any contact. And, yes, he earned his reputation over the years, but I didn't realize he was philandering while he was still married to her," she said. "I'm not ready to forgive her but I'm also realizing how complicated family dynamics can be. Now I'm thinking that maybe she had good reason to leave and not look back." Ella shot a compassionate look.

"I can't argue that families are complex." Madelyn still hadn't figured out what to say to her own father. She picked up the heavy tray, balanced it on her shoulder and walked into the other room behind Ella.

THE LUNCH PLATES were cleared and Madelyn hadn't said two words since going into the kitchen with Ella earlier. Hudson had hoped they'd come to some kind of truce in there but Madelyn returned looking even more stressed. Coffee was served and he took a sip. One look at Madelyn said it was time to wrap this up.

Hudson made a move to stand but Ed Staples waved at him. "Please. Wait. I know it took a great deal of courage for Madelyn to come here today and I also know she has something to ask of the family."

The twins got that "here goes" look on their faces at exactly the same moment.

"I'd like a DNA test for clarification," Madelyn said, wasting no time.

Hudson took another sip of coffee, needing the caffeine boost. Since Madelyn had come to stay with him, things were stirring inside him. Common sense dictated that should make him want her to leave. He didn't.

The twin who'd identified himself as Dalton chuckled and Madelyn shot him a severe look. It looked a helluva lot like the one Ella fired at him and Hudson tried not to read too much into it. He glanced at the picture on the wall of Mike Butler. There was a resemblance.

Dalton held up both hands in the sign of surrender. "Hey. Don't get angry with me. I'm just laughing that you think the old man would make something like this up."

"I didn't know your father, so I have no idea what he would do and why," Madelyn defended.

"Then allow me to apologize. Suffice it to say that my...*our*...old man wouldn't take a claim like this lightly," Dalton clarified. "If he says you're one of us then I'd be shocked if a DNA test proved otherwise."

"That may be true, but I'd still like to know for sure," she said. "I don't want your money or the ranch. I just want to know."

The other twin, who had been quiet up until now, leaned forward and rested his elbows on his knees. "No offense but once it's established that you're a Butler—and my brother is right, by the way, our father wouldn't utter those words if they weren't true—you'll have every right to his money and the ranch. And none of us would stand in the way of his wishes."

Dalton was rocking his head in agreement.

The twins were stand-up men. Ella seemed a little put off that Madelyn rejected her heritage so easily.

"Which one of us do you want to swab?" Ella asked. "Or would you like one from all three to be absolutely certain?"

"One should suffice," Madelyn said. "But how do we proceed? I mean, I want to make sure the results aren't tampered with and I haven't exactly had time to figure all this out."

That comment netted a few angry looks.

"We aren't going to sabotage your test," Dalton said. "But you should learn to trust us. We aren't the self-absorbed jerks the media makes us out to be."

Madelyn tensed. "Not all of us in the media are like the people out there. Some of us expose truths that should be known, that help others."

"Hold on a damn second," Dalton said. "You're one of them?"

"I believe I just said that I wasn't, but, yes, I'm an investigative reporter."

He pushed his chair back and stood. "I'm done here. And, for the record, everything we just said is unofficial. If I see one word of this in print—"

Hudson didn't like where this was going, so he pushed to his feet. If a table wasn't separating them, he and Dalton would be nose to nose, given they were almost equal height. "She's not here for that reason and we all know it, so cool it."

All the warmth in the room disappeared and all three of the Butler children tensed as though ready for a fight. He could give one thing to them: they stuck together.

"She wants something everyone deserves, and that's to know who her father is. Before Ed Staples called and turned her life upside down, she believed it was the man she'd grown up with. Her mother is gone, so she can't ask her," he stated. "So, you guys hold the key."

Ella stood. Her expression was calm but he suspected it was like the surface of water on the stove just before the boiling point was reached. "Ed can arrange everything. You can work with him on the details. We'll comply. In the meantime, I can have a room set up for you here at the ranch. As a Butler, you'll have a right to stay anytime you want."

Why did that offer twist Hudson's gut?

"Do you want to stay here?"

Chapter Thirteen

"My car's at your place," Madelyn responded to Hudson. She couldn't read his expression. Did he want her to stay with the Butlers? He'd been the one pushing her to come and find answers—answers she wanted but also threatened to shake her foundation to the core.

"It's your call." She searched his face and found nothing to give away his thoughts. His grip was pretty tight on his mug.

"I could stay if it's easier on you," she said, knowing full well it wasn't safe for her to go to a motel in town. But then, a Butler could be targeting her. Sure, they seemed sincere and just as surprised as she had been to learn the news of her possible heritage. On the other hand, she didn't know Ella, Dade or Dalton personally. Any one of them could be putting on a show. Yes, they were convincing and seemed welcoming under the circumstances. Didn't mean they weren't plotting behind her back to get rid of her.

"We still haven't spoken to Kelsey or located Trent. I'd like to hear what they have to say and then there's the vandalism with your car we still haven't reported," Hudson said after a long pause. He was curious about the investigation? "Might be easier to stay put at my place since all your things are already there."

Her heart leaped.

"What's been going on?" Ella asked, a frown of worry apparent on her face. After what she'd been through, it made sense that she'd be concerned.

Madelyn flashed her eyes at Ed. She hadn't

told the lawyer. "When did you tell everyone about me?"

"Last night. Why?" Ella cut in.

"Someone tried to stop me from coming here after Ed called," Madelyn said, her attention on Ella now.

Ella drew back and gasped. "Are you all right?" She waved her hands in the air. "Never mind that. I can see you're not physically hurt."

Madelyn relayed the details of the incident on the road and the threat on the mirror.

"Is that why you checked out of Red Rope?" Ed said.

Madelyn's brow shot up and he quickly reassured her.

"I was simply trying to locate you and you weren't answering your cell. I called the front desk, asking to be connected to your room, and they said you weren't staying with them," he clarified.

"Don't look at us," Dade said. "We've been

here on lockdown. Ella throws a fit every time one of us so much as tries to leave the ranch."

"We have to take this seriously," Ella said, lines of anxiety etched in her forehead. "I'd like you to stay here where we can be sure you're safe."

"With all due respect, your father was killed on this property," Hudson reminded her.

"Not in the main house. And we've tightened security since then," Ella said. Her demeanor changed the second she'd learned of the threat. "This might not mean much coming from me right now, but I'd like to know that you're safe. No matter what the DNA test reveals—and my money's on the fact that it'll prove what you don't want to hear—I feel like we're responsible."

"How so?" Madelyn asked.

"You said this whole thing started after the call from Ed," Ella said. "If his call triggered this, someone might be listening to our calls."

She looked at her brothers. "Is that even possible?"

"Anything goes with technology these days if someone's savvy enough," Dade said. "I'll let Ray Canton know." He looked to Madelyn and said, "He heads up security here at Hereford. He'll be able to tell us if the signal can be unscrambled."

"If someone picked up on Ed's call, they must know what's going on," Ella said.

Hudson reached for her hand, found it. Madelyn wound their fingers together.

"I didn't tell her over the phone," Ed admitted. "Your father had an envelope in a safe in his office. She's the only one who knew the contents once she opened it."

"You already knew," Madelyn countered.

"I had my suspicions. Mike Butler and I go way back. I knew your mother," he said with an apologetic look to Ella and the twins.

But Madelyn had locked onto that last bit…

"How well did you know my mother?" she asked.

"Well enough to know that she isn't from Houston. Your father moved there after she passed away." He seemed to choose his next words carefully. "The minute I saw you, my suspicions were confirmed. You looked exactly how I picture a child of theirs would."

Madelyn wasn't sure if that was a compliment, and she was grateful for the link with Hudson. Their connected hands were the only thing keeping her balanced. "Did you see proof?"

"No. Just what my eyes knew."

"So, it's possible that I'm not his daughter," Madelyn said. At this point, she wasn't sure what she wanted to be true. If she was Butler's illegitimate child then her father's actions were understandable. It would make sense that he'd kept her at a distance her entire life. Otherwise, she had to consider the possibility—

the one she'd wholeheartedly feared before this revelation—that her own father didn't love her.

Was that true?

She stood and glanced around the room. It seemed to shrink, the walls closing in. "I need fresh air."

Not one to wait for permission, she darted toward the door and burst outside. The August sun on her face warmed her skin. The blast of heat made it harder to breathe, though. She heard a pair of boots shuffling behind her and was comforted by the fact that Hudson had followed her.

"We don't have to stick around," he said. "We'll get the swab and go."

Madelyn tried to speak but her mouth snapped shut. There was so much she wanted to say, so much that had been bottled up inside ever since she'd heard the news—news that still seemed too crazy to be true. "All my life I've been told my mother was this...*saint*...and I held her up here." She lifted her flat palm as far as she could above her head. "I had this image of her being an angel and looking over me."

"Kids have a way of idolizing a parent who has passed away," he said, and his voice was low. He was standing right behind her. She felt his strong hands on her shoulders and her body responded.

"You can say that again," she said on a sharp sigh. "Anytime I had a bad day—and there were plenty of those, especially in high school when a girl needs her mother—I'd curl up under the covers and envision her holding me. I literally envisioned her with wings, for crying out loud. Now I guess I'm the fool. Not only was my mother no saint but she had an affair with one married man and tricked another guy into marrying her."

"How can you be so sure that your father didn't know?" he asked.

"Because if he knew that explains why he'd

been so cold to me all my life. Why he let me cry it out in my room instead of comforting me when I was upset." Her pulse pounded, part anger and part awareness of the strong hands gripping her shoulders. "It explains why he only calls once a month instead of every day. And it explains why he doesn't love me."

Those last few words were daggers to the heart.

Hudson spun her around to face him and she couldn't look into his eyes. She didn't want to see her reflection there—because in his eyes she felt beautiful and loved. More of what she wanted to see instead of reality.

"I haven't met the man, so I'll reserve judgment until I do. But if he turned his back on you or didn't love you it's his loss, not yours." His words were a warm blanket on a frigid night. "You're smart and determined. You have a sense of humor on top of heart-stopping beauty."

Did he just say she was beautiful? Her heart gave a little flip as she struggled against the hot tears burning the backs of her eyes.

"If he really is my father, what does it say about me that he doesn't love me?" The words spoken aloud ripped a hole in her chest.

"Impossible." He ran his thumb along her jawline and sensual shivers rocked her body.

"Maybe not." She dared to look up and his gaze seemed to look right through her.

"We agreed not to do this again, but I'd like permission to kiss you." His brown eyes darkened with need.

Madelyn pushed up on her tiptoes and pressed her lips to his in answer. This wasn't the time for words.

Hudson deepened the kiss, his tongue delving inside, tasting her, and he groaned. He brought his hands up to cup her face and need pulsed through her.

As if realizing they were standing on the Butlers' front lawn in full view of the family, he pulled back. "I won't say it."

"You don't have to. We both know it's true but I want to enjoy this moment anyway," she said.

His quick nod affirmed they were on the same page. They stood there, knowing this couldn't go further, and yet unwilling to let the moment end. He was so close that she could smell the coffee on his breath and remembered the taste of it a few seconds ago. He pressed his forehead to hers and took in a deep breath. "If I could go there with anyone… I would. I hope you know that. There's too much back there and I can't shake it."

"I know." He referred to being able to talk about his past.

"I haven't been in love in a long time. And now I can't," he continued.

"You don't have to explain it to me. I understand more than you realize." There was only so far she could go with a man, any man, and they'd reached that wall. Hudson scared her even more because she could almost envision herself busting down that barrier with him. But shatter it and then what? Hudson wasn't ready to let her in. They both had issues. Not to mention the fact that she had someone trying to run her out of town…possibly *kill* her.

All this emotion could be that they were two lost souls, searching for a temporary reprieve from almost constant pain.

"Being rejected by my father hurt. Losing my mother hurt. All I know is heartache," she said, figuring that she was a magnet, drawing hurt toward her like the scent of honey draws bees. Let the swarm turn on her and it would be all over.

He lifted her chin until their gazes collided. "You deserve so much more than that."

But he'd already admitted that he wasn't the

one who could give it to her. And her stubborn heart said it needed him.

She blinked up at him. "We should get back inside."

There was no use trying to convince him that they might be able to give it a shot. She'd tried to make someone love her for her entire life. Granted, it was a whole different kind of love, but that didn't seem important to her at the moment.

"We should tell them we're leaving," he said, letting go of her and taking a step back. The sharp breath he drew seemed meant to steel his strength.

Part of Madelyn wanted to get lost in him, to forget everything that had happened recently. She couldn't do that any more than she could change her identity with a quick revelation from Maverick Mike Butler. No matter how much her heart protested.

As she started toward the door, it swung

open. Ella Butler stood there, flanked by her brothers. They stood more relaxed now and almost seemed sympathetic.

"Ed is arranging the DNA test, unless you want to oversee it," Ella said. "He's planning to expedite the results. I'm sure you don't want to be in limbo any longer than you have to be."

No one mentioned how the result might change things for Madelyn—for all of them, actually. Instead, they all seemed poised to respect her privacy.

"I'm fine with Ed taking the lead," Madelyn said. He had no vested interest in the outcome and seemed to genuinely care about Mike Butler's wishes. There were other pressing questions she wanted to ask him but decided none of them mattered until she received confirmation of what she suspected, feared, to be true.

"He has a kit waiting in the kitchen. We've already been swabbed." She twisted her face into a frown. "If you want us to do it again with you present, we can."

"That won't be necessary." Madelyn needed to establish a little trust. It was tentative at best on both sides, but the family seemed to be making an effort and she should, too. Besides, there was a slight possibility that they would be connected for the rest of their lives and she couldn't ignore it.

She followed Ella and the twins into the kitchen.

"Could I have a minute with Ed?" she asked.

Everyone nodded and left, except Hudson. She'd asked him to stay.

"You said you knew my mother," Madelyn said to Ed.

He stood next to her at the grand wooden table positioned in the middle of the room. His body language was tense, his shoulders rigid and the lines on his face deep.

"Yes, ma'am. I had the pleasure of meeting

her a couple of times," he said, and there was so much respect in his voice.

"Can you tell me something about her?" Madelyn wanted—no, needed—to know, and Ed seemed the only one willing to talk about her mother even if his body language said he was reluctant.

"She had your hair and eyes," he said. That, she could gain from a picture.

"What was she like?" Madelyn tried to quell the hope in her voice but was doing a lousy job, by all counts.

Ed gave her a shocked look.

"My father—" she flashed her eyes at him "—her husband never said much about her."

"The loss was probably too difficult," Ed said, but there wasn't a lot of conviction in his tone.

"What was she like? Did she have a sense of humor?" she asked, guiding the discussion back on track.

Ed looked up and to the right, like he was searching deep for memories of her. His gaze shifted, landing on Madelyn. "You have her smile. I know that because she always wore hers. Her laugh could fill a room and she was so darn pretty that it was hard to catch your breath when she walked in."

Madelyn had never considered herself to be that beautiful. Except in Hudson's presence. There, she felt like the most beautiful woman in the room.

"Forgive my saying so, but she didn't take life as seriously as you do," he said.

Maybe her mother hadn't been forced to. Madelyn, on the other hand, had lost her mother at birth and grown up with a father who was loving in his own way and unyielding. She'd learned to work hard at an early age and there'd been no silliness allowed. Coddling, according to her father, would spoil her. He was preparing her for adulthood. And it had begun as early as she could remember.

The contrast between Charles Kensington and her mother, Arabella, struck her. Didn't people say that opposites attracted? If her mother was really that much of a free spirit, then she and Charles, with his rigid view of life, couldn't be more contrary.

"Did she go to church?"

Ed laughed.

Madelyn wondered if that part had been made up so she would ask fewer questions. She'd viewed her mother as a saint and her father, Charles, had taken the easy road by delivering exactly what she'd wanted to hear. Madelyn had been beating herself up pretty hard for her mistakes. Somehow, knowing how imperfect her mother had been lifted some of the heavy weight on Madelyn's shoulders.

"Sorry. I don't mean any disrespect, but your mother wasn't the religious type. She had a zest for life and church would've given her too many rules. She would've found that way too restrictive." There was so much admiration in his eyes when he spoke about her mother.

"What about this? Why did Mike Butler give it to her?" She toyed with the dragonfly around her neck.

"Ah. I was wondering when you would ask about that," he said with a smile, handing her a cotton swab.

Madelyn took the offering and rolled it around inside her cheek, careful to coat it well. She didn't want the test to come back inconclusive.

Ed nodded toward the necklace as he opened a Ziploc-style baggie. She dropped in the specimen and he immediately sealed it.

"She loved collecting dragonflies," he continued. "She'd go on and on about their magical qualities, something to do with them giving a deeper understanding of life, of self. She felt like they were powerful and graceful at the same time." He blinked. "A bit like you, if you don't mind me saying."

Madelyn tried not to let that thought comfort her. It did. The thought that her mother wouldn't see her as a disappointment let sunshine into dark places inside her heart.

"She'd light up when she talked about them," he continued. "She'd talk about how fast they could move and it was something like thirty or forty miles an hour. But they could also hover like a helicopter and fly backward if they really wanted. But the thing she liked best about them was how simple and elegant they were, like a ballerina, she'd say. She thought they had some kind of mystical wisdom and would always bring light to her."

"Guess it didn't work out so well," she said and instantly regretted it when the sad look crossed Ed's worn features.

"From what I hear, she'd been forbidden to wear it while she gave birth," he said.

"So, my father knew?" She couldn't hide her shock.

"About the necklace? Yes. I assume he was told the rest." Ed looked her in the eyes and she could see that he was being honest.

"What about Mike Butler? Did he know right away or find out later?" She might as well go for it.

"My guess, and this is only a guess, is that he knew."

A fire lit inside her. A man like Mike Butler could afford a better hospital. Check that, could afford *the best* medical care. Her mother had died because of a negligent county hospital. She could be alive right now if he hadn't abandoned her. He'd turned his back on his daughter, too. If the paternity test turned out positive, he'd left her to be brought up by a man who could never truly love her while his four legitimate children grew up with all this. She and her father had struggled to make ends meet. "So, he didn't love my mother?"

"My friend was a complicated man. I believe that he did love your mother. He'd been talking about leaving MaryAnn, his wife." His gaze shifted to the floor. "Their marriage had been on the rocks and, looking back, it was just as much his fault as hers. He liked to drink and still had wild oats to sow. MaryAnn turned up pregnant and I thought that's why he stayed with her. The only thing my friend ever said when I asked about your mother was that she said she was in love with another man," he said.

"And Mike Butler, a man used to getting everything he wanted, left it at that?" She didn't believe that for a second. "He doesn't sound like the kind of man who was used to letting someone else get his way."

"She married Charles Kensington. What else

could he do?" Ed said on a wistful-sounding sigh.

A man she didn't love, would never love.

"But then she died and Mike just left his child for another man to bring up." She couldn't mask the hurt in her voice.

"He visited Charles, asking to see you. The two had words that I was never privileged to hear and Mike left it alone," he stated.

Maverick Mike visited her father? She couldn't imagine how that discussion had gone down. Her hope that her father, Charles, didn't know that she was an illegitimate child was dying a slow death. The question was more like, how could he *not* have known? More questions joined. Why would he keep her? What did he have to gain by bringing up another man's child? Had Maverick Mike bribed her father? Pawned her off on him?

And then she thought about Charles's small business. He'd done okay for a small-time operation. But he hadn't been able to save enough to pay for her college and they'd lived on a shoestring budget. It had taken him years to pay off the hospital bill and he'd insisted on paying every last penny. She'd worked her way through college and had the student loans to prove it.

Thinking about the picture in the dining room with the wealthy smiling family filled her with anger. She had Mike's nose and even she couldn't argue that he was most likely her father. There was absolutely no way she was ready to accept the fact just yet. But that didn't make it less true.

The conversation she needed to have with Charles Kensington couldn't wait.

"Are we done here?" she asked Ed.

He nodded.

She turned to Hudson. "Ready to go?"

"Yes." He put his hand on the small of her

back and she couldn't allow the comfort his touch provided.

Ignoring the electricity pinging between them, she led him to his pickup truck parked out front. The grip she had on her cell phone should've cracked the protective case. She climbed into the passenger seat and stared at her contact list. Her finger hovered over the word *Dad*.

She pushed the button as Hudson took the driver's seat.

The phone rang once, twice and then three times. She had no plans to let her father off the hook this time.

His voice-mail recording began and she pushed the button to bypass it.

"I know who my real father is." Madelyn ended the call before her voice could break.

She waited thirty seconds and called again.

"Pull over," Madelyn said to Hudson when her father picked up.

Chapter Fourteen

Hudson made a nosedive for an empty parking lot next to a field. As soon as the truck stopped, Madelyn hopped out and started pacing. She couldn't sit still and take this call. She needed to be moving.

"I know everything, Father. Or should I say Charles?" she asked, not bothering to mask her bitterness. There'd been too many opportunities for him to tell her, to make this right over the years, and he'd chosen to keep her in the dark.

The line was silent.

"What? Don't you have anything to say to me

after all these years? Thirty years of flat-out lies?" Her body trembled with pent-up frustration—frustration that was seeking release with no outlet.

A quick glance at Hudson revealed he was leaning against the truck, arms folded, ankles crossed.

"Why don't you come to Friday supper and we can talk about this?" her father said, his calm voice both comforting and infuriating at the same time. Charles Kensington was not an emotional man.

"First of all, someone's after me because I'm a Butler, and the worst part about it all is that I didn't even know I was a Butler. Ridiculous me thought I was a Kensington all this time," she blurted out.

The line was so quiet that she thought her father had ended the call. She wanted to scream, to shout, to get something out of the man to show that he had a beating heart in that ice-cold chest of his.

"You don't sound like you feel well. We should talk when you're better," he said, and she got a lot of pleasure out of a small fracture in his tone.

"How about after I'm dead, like my mother," she shot back, unable to contain the fire in hers.

"It's bad manners to talk derogatory about someone who has passed," he said, regaining that tight lip.

"How so, *Dad*?" She was waving a red flag in the face of a determined bull. In her father's case, the bull was determined not to show any emotion. Par for the course and more proof that he didn't care.

"Should I set an extra place at the table?" he asked.

"Are you kidding me? Don't bother. I won't be coming home ever again. Because you're not my father and I don't want to have anything to do with lies." That should get him riled up.

It didn't.

"Have it your way. Call if you change your mind. Otherwise, there isn't much more to say."

The line died and her heart fisted as the crack of a bullet split the air.

It took a few seconds to register what had happened. A few more to come to grips with the reality someone had fired at them. All of which came too late because the shooter got off another round as Hudson tackled her, covering her with his considerable size as she flew to the hard concrete. Her head almost cracked against the pavement, but Hudson shielded it.

"Stay low," Hudson said, popping up to all fours.

Madelyn rolled over onto her stomach and belly-crawled toward the truck. She barely registered the pain in her hands at clawing across the pavement filled with tiny jagged rocks.

This wasn't the time to worry about the ache shooting through her knees.

Hudson muttered the same curse she was thinking as another shot fired. The ping sound of a bullet hitting metal on the truck sent an icy chill racing up her spine. Fear gripped her as Hudson's arm came around her, his hand on her stomach, and lifted her into the passenger seat.

"Keep your head down, eyes below the dashboard," he said sharply. "Get into as small of a ball as you can on the floorboard."

Madelyn did as he climbed over her and into the driver's side. The door closed behind him and the next second he was gunning the motor. She remembered the shotgun tucked behind the seat. She could reach it and fire off a few shots, giving them the distance they needed to outrun the shooter, or she could hide.

"Do you know anyone who owns a rifle?" Hudson asked.

"Yes—more than half the state, according to statistics," she said and then made her move.

"I told you to stay down," Hudson shouted.

"You can't drive and shoot. I'm not helpless. I won't cower on the floorboard when I can make a difference," she stated. "Where's the ammunition?"

"There in the dash," Hudson said.

She bounced around in the seat but managed to gain purchase on the butt of the shotgun. Next, she located a shell and loaded it. "Who am I shooting at?"

"White sedan. It's the only vehicle behind us."

Hands shaking from a burst of adrenaline, Madelyn opened the little window between the cab and the truck bed, took aim and fired.

The sedan swerved and the driver must've hit the brakes because the hood dipped as the car slowed. She loaded another shell and pumped the action, hoping to blow out a tire this time.

From the looks of things, she missed entirely, but the main goal was to slow down the driver so that they could slip away, and that had been accomplished. He backed off and pulled onto the shoulder.

She kept her gaze focused on the sedan until it disappeared completely from view. "He's gone."

"Call the sheriff," Hudson said with more than a hint of admiration in his voice. "Tell him to come to the ranch. Talking to your father will have to wait."

By the time he parked in his garage, she'd given her statement to the sheriff. And it was probably because she'd almost died—again!— that her heart rate was jacked through the roof, or maybe it was the compassion he'd shown earlier and the constant reminders that someone wanted to kill her, but Madelyn climbed over the seat and onto Hudson's lap.

Before he reminded her that this was a bad

idea or brought them both back to their senses, she kissed him. The heat in that kiss robbed her breath as she tunneled her fingers into his thick hair.

There was so much heat roaring through her body, seeking an outlet, that her body ached. Ached with need for Hudson. She needed to feel him moving inside her and needed the bliss that would follow getting completely lost with him. She needed to feel her naked skin against his strong, hard body.

He smelled of coffee and outdoors and spice. Just the scent of him turned her on and had her craving *more*. More of him. More of this moment. Just more until they rose to the sky before exploding into a thousand pieces of light and drifting to the earth like confetti during a celebration parade.

His hands searched her body, roaming over her stomach.

And the next thing she realized was the door

to the truck flying open and Hudson wrapping his hands around her bottom as he twisted around until his boots were on the pavement. He carried her to the front door, couldn't seem to get the key in the lock fast enough, and then rushed inside. He kicked the door closed and then spun around until her back was against it. She found the lock, making sure they were safe. His body was flush with hers, her legs wrapped around his midsection, and she could feel his thick erection pulsing, denim against denim.

"You're beautiful," he said as he planted kisses along her neck. His hot breath sliding through her, causing a deep well of need to rise from within.

"So are you," she said, and he laughed, his chest rumbling against her body.

She matched his enthusiasm. His lips found hers and she thrust her tongue in his mouth. He groaned as his hands cupped her bottom and he pressed harder against her.

All she could do was surrender to the flames engulfing her. Madelyn gripped both of Hudson's shoulders and he pulled back enough to look her in the eyes.

"We're wearing far too many clothes," she said.

"You're sure this is a good idea?" he asked, the hunger in his gaze almost feral. His voice was low, husky and sexy.

Madelyn answered by urging her feet to the floor and pulling the hem of her blouse over her head.

His tongue slicked across his bottom lip and he groaned as his eyes roamed her body, hungry, seeking. He brought his hand up, using his index finger to outline her lacy bra. Her nipples pebbled and her breasts swelled under his touch.

He cupped her breasts and she reached in back for the release. He slid the straps over her shoulders, groaning again when her breasts were free. He dipped his head and captured her nipple in his mouth. Her body ached for him to touch more. His tongue slicked a hot trail circling around her nipple until he took her in his mouth.

Madelyn tugged at the hem of his T-shirt and he aided her in removing it with one swift motion. Her hands were already on the fastener of his jeans by the time his joined hers. He fumbled with one of the buttons as his hands trembled with the same need coursing through her.

Their rapid breaths mingled and she was ready to taste him. So, she did. Madelyn dropped down to her knees and gripped his length after he stepped out of his denim. She teased his tip with her tongue, drawing a guttural groan from deep in his chest. Working her hand along the shaft as she alternately licked and teased caused his muscles to cord.

"We need to slow down," he said, and she liked being the one in control.

She eased her closed hand around him, sliding up and down in unison with her tongue. And when she brought him to the brink, he helped her up and out of her jeans.

"Hold on," he said, disappearing for a second down the hallway and returning with a condom already secured. His body was perfection as he moved, his muscles flexing and releasing with every intentional stride toward her.

Madelyn had already slid her panties off and tossed them with the pile of clothes on the floor.

Hudson was making a beeline toward her and her heart stuttered at the hungry look on his face. She wrapped her arms around him as soon as he was close and he picked her up. She expected him to ease into her but instead he walked her over to the massive handmade wooden table and cleared it in one swipe. With her back on the table, he trailed kisses down her neck, around her breasts and then farther down still. Down her stomach toward her wet heat. He drove his tongue inside her as he worked her mound with his fingers. Her back arched as pleasure rippled through her from her thighs to her crown as he brought her closer to the tipping point.

When she couldn't take it any longer, she tugged him over her, loving the feel of his muscled body on top of her, pressing her back into the table. She wrapped her legs around his toned stomach as he dipped his tip inside her heat. She was so ready for him, and the second he realized it, he drove himself deep inside. She moaned as the electric current pinging inside her reached fever pitch with each long stride.

Her fingers dug into his shoulders as she tried to brace herself for the moment when she would soar over the edge. His pace was frantic and she matched each stroke until they both exploded in an inferno of bliss as bombs detonated inside her. She could feel his length pulsing as he reached the same sweet release until all that was left inside them were heavy breaths.

She didn't say that was amazing, but it was. In fact, that was the best sex of her life, and it was so much more than the physical act. The emotional connection she felt brought it to a whole new level, and she hoped—maybe sensed—he had the same experience.

His lips found hers and she got lost in that sensation of being with Hudson. And then he gently wrapped his arms around her bottom as she put her arms around his neck. He lifted her and held her tight as he brought her to his bedroom.

The bed was easily large enough for two people and the room was comfortably furnished. But that was not what she was focused on. All she could think about was how right she felt in his arms and how much she'd needed that release to break the sexual current that had been sizzling between them since she first met him.

She dressed in time for the sheriff to show up and then take their statements.

But when she got back into bed and pulled up the covers, she didn't think about being shot at or the white sedan.

She thought about Hudson as she fell into a deep sleep.

HUDSON PUT ON a pot of coffee. Seven hours was the most sleep he'd gotten since…

He didn't want to go there. Not after having the best sex of his life and especially not after his heart stirred in ways it hadn't in… He paused. Ever.

A wave of guilt crashed into him. He muttered a curse under his breath. The last thing he wanted to think about was the past when he'd had a short reprieve while he was with Madelyn and, for once, he felt good.

"What's wrong?" Madelyn said from the doorway. The sound of her voice shocked him out of his reverie. He turned toward her and the shot that pierced him was like a bullet to the heart. It also told him that he was in deep trouble. It was too soon to try to figure out what exactly that meant.

"Nothing," he lied, making a straight line toward her and not stopping until she was in his arms and he'd kissed her. All he could think about now was just how shattered he'd been after they'd made love and how much he was ready to do it again.

She pushed up to her tiptoes to deepen the kiss and that was all the encouragement he needed to pick her up and take her back to bed.

They'd made love at a frantic pace last night and this time he wanted to take his time, explore her body and feel her soft creamy skin against his. He broke off the kiss long enough to place a condom on his tip and she rolled it down his shaft for him. All he could think was how much trouble he was in because he couldn't get enough of the wheat-haired beauty as she straddled him and pushed him down on the bed.

This time, she climbed on top of him and set the pace. Long, slow strokes caused the tension to build inside him until he was on the edge again. Her pert breasts bounced as she rode him, and his hands roamed her flat stomach before gripping her sweet bottom. He could feel the tension building inside her as she increased her speed, grinding her sex on top of him. The sweet feel of her muscles tightening around him and her body cording with tension until she exploded in sweet release.

He flipped her onto her back and she smiled up at him—right then he knew that he was a goner. Once, twice… Hell, three times would never be enough.

She pulled him down on top of her, wrapped her legs around him and he drove himself home. It might be temporary, but it was home.

Chapter Fifteen

Madelyn woke reaching for Hudson and felt cold sheets instead where he'd been. The sun was bright in the sky and she couldn't believe it when she checked the clock and realized that she'd slept until ten thirty, a luxury she couldn't remember when she'd indulged last. She stretched, feeling the happy soreness that always seemed to accompany multiple rounds of back-to-back good sex. *Really* good sex. Okay, mind-blowing sex. And something else?

The feeling was foreign because she'd never been this connected to anyone else or felt this at home. Heck, her own place didn't make her feel this safe and comfortable. Ever since this whole episode with Owen had started, she'd been lucky to get five hours of sleep in a row. And before that, needing to find the truth, to give others answers she'd never known, had driven her to work fourteen-hour days. Her father popped into her thoughts. She needed to circle back and speak to him. She didn't like the way they'd left things. He had been her dad for almost three decades.

Coffee. She needed coffee. She didn't need to overanalyze her life and especially not whatever was happening between her and Hudson. Her heart tried to argue but a strong need for caffeine momentarily silenced all protests. She threw on Hudson's white button-down collared shirt, the one that had been flung over the chair in his room, and fastened a couple of buttons.

A pot was already on, so she poured a cup. The hot liquid burned her throat in the best possible way as she took her first sip. Palming her mug, enjoying the warmth, she moved toward the window to see if she could see him. He was most likely feeding animals, checking the fence for breaks or exercising his horse, Bullseye.

She located him almost immediately in the practice ring, and watched the grace with which the animal and rider moved. Thoughts of the feel of his rugged hands all over her skin brought a tingling sensation to her arms. She moved to the screened-in patio on the back porch, enjoying the bright sunshine and the beauty of the land.

There was something right about being here. Madelyn didn't want to get inside her head about what that meant. She just sat there, admiring the ease with which Hudson guided his horse around the ring. She was on her second cup when her stomach decided food needed to be a priority. It took great effort to force herself up off the comfortable Adirondack chair.

She fluffed the pillow and picked up her empty mug, not quite ready to leave the quiet, the stillness of the place. Because she was calm on the inside and she hadn't experienced that since long before Owen. Probably never when she really thought about it and she was reluctant to let this moment end.

She lingered, looking out onto the land.

As she scanned the horizon, she saw someone about Owen's size and build stalking toward Hudson from the tree line. Her heart leaped to her throat. At first, she thought she was seeing things. It couldn't be him. And even if it was, how would Owen know where she was?

A dark feeling came over her as she watched the figure move toward the exercise ring. Did he have something in his hand? A weapon?

She flew to the screen door, flung it open and screamed at Hudson. Her finger was pointed directly at the approaching figure when he looked at her. He froze for a split second before spinning around and retreating.

Hudson wasted no time breaking his horse out of the corral. A shot was fired, and to Bullseye's credit, he didn't panic. Hudson had to stop long enough to open the gate but he was skilled on horseback and broke his mare into a full run toward the trees, aiming Bullseye at the spot she'd indicated. Her heart galloped at the thought he was heading toward the danger. She scanned his white T-shirt for signs of blood.

The figure had disappeared. She searched the trees, looking for any sign of him. He could be anywhere. She regretted yelling out in panic. If she'd kept a cool head, she might've been able to sneak up on him. And then do what? Confront a man who had a gun?

Another shot rang out and Madelyn gasped. Instinct took over and she dropped down to all fours.

If it was Owen, and she couldn't confirm that it was, he'd lost his mind if he followed her to Cattle Barge. Hudson and Bullseye had disappeared into the trees and her heart free-fell at the possibility he wouldn't come out.

It seemed like forever but was probably only ten or fifteen minutes by the time Hudson emerged. He and his horse broke from the tree line at a solid trot. She ran toward them, desperately searching his shirt for blood, but Hudson motioned for her to go back.

"Stay in the house," he shouted. He hopped off his horse and secured Bullseye before dashing onto the porch. "What did you see?"

"A man about my ex's height and build," she started.

"Was it him?"

"I can't be certain. I mean, a lot of men are around five foot ten and a hundred fifty pounds, right?"

Hudson nodded.

"He could come back, couldn't he?" She hated the way her voice trembled.

"Yes. And we'll be ready for him." His jaw ticked.

"How? You can't stay awake all the time and this whole situation is escalating." Her fingers twisted thinking about the danger she'd put him in. "Maybe I should go to the Butler ranch. You could come with me."

He paused like he was considering it. "I can't leave my horses."

"Could Doris stay with them?" Madelyn already knew the answer. He would never risk involving another person, and neither would she, now that she really thought about it. She was having a knee-jerk reaction and needed to calm down so she could think clearly.

Her ringtone sounded in the other room.

"I better answer that." She dashed into the kitchen and located her cell. *Owen.* "You're not supposed to call me anymore."

"I have to see you," he said, and she listened for any signs of him being out of breath or sounds of nature in the background. If it had been him a little while ago, there'd be something to give him away. Right? Owen was sneaky, a little voice reminded her.

"We both know that's not going to happen." A frustrated sigh slipped out when she could detect nothing. It couldn't have been him. There was no way he'd be this calm and there was no noise other than a TV.

"It doesn't have to be this way, Madelyn. I mean, the restraining order. I was a jerk and said things I didn't mean. I'll never make that mistake again. If you say it's over and you're done I'll respect it. But at least see me one more time," he begged. There was more than a hint of desperation in his tone.

"You're right. We didn't have to get to this place. But this was the path you chose and you need to explain yourself to a judge. If he thinks you should get off for what you did, that's up to him. I'm not withdrawing the court order."

"It's a mistake on your part." Was he threatening her? Again?

"Believe me when I tell you that you need to leave it alone. Walk away," she said.

"I can't. We'll see each other again," he stated.

Didn't that send creepy crawlies down her spine?

"If that was you, Owen, you need to cut it out. Keep your distance or you'll have even more to regret," she warned.

"What are you talking about?" He was either a very good actor or he really didn't know. With Owen, she couldn't be sure.

"I'm telling you to stay away from me," she spelled out for him.

"What do you think I'm doing now?" he shot back. There was a lot of confidence in his tone and that had her leaning toward the trespasser being someone else. But who? One of the Butlers? Someone from the media? A fresh wave of panic washed over her. Another thought struck. Trent?

"Violating a court order," she stated.

"That, I'm not doing. Madelyn, it's me. We had something good together. Don't ruin it now with all this legal mess. Just have dinner with me and we'll talk it out. You'll see that I'm ready and willing to respect your boundaries."

A frustrated sound tore from her throat. "Like you are right now?"

"I'm sorry," he said. "And you're right. I'm trying to get you to agree to see me and here I am being a total jerk. But it's only because I still care about you. That has to be a little charming, right?"

She wasn't about to fall into that trap with him. "I already said that's not possible. Contact me through your attorney from now on."

"You're going to regret this, Madelyn," he said, all the charm in his voice long gone.

"The only regret I have is getting involved with you in the first place, Owen."

The line went dead.

"Who was that?" Hudson asked, startling her.

"Owen."

Hudson's hands fisted at his sides. "Wish you'd let me talk to him."

She had no doubt that Hudson wouldn't take lightly a man who threatened women. "I'm trying to let the law handle him."

"Where was he?" Hudson was most likely thinking along the same lines as her.

"I heard a TV in the background and he wasn't out of breath." She wished there'd been more clues.

"Doesn't rule him out."

"Have you heard word from the sheriff today?" she asked.

"There's no news of the white sedan." Hudson moved to the coffee maker. "You want a cup?"

"I'd like that. Can we take it to go? There's someone I need to talk to this morning."

EVERYTHING WAS HOT this time of year in Texas, from the sidewalks to the rooftops. Lack of rain had left large cracks in the front yard of the house where Madelyn had grown up. She wondered how smart it was to build houses on dry, shifty soil.

She climbed the couple of stairs onto the four-by-four cement porch of her childhood home. She couldn't count the number of times she'd returned since leaving for college. There'd been many. She'd spent so many days of her young life playing on this very porch, in this yard.

Looking around, she found that everything appeared different this time. The place seemed smaller and the flowers out front needed a good watering.

Before she could reach for the handle, the front door flew open.

Charles, her father, stood there. She'd never once seen him get emotional and yet his puffy eyes were glassy and red as though he'd been crying.

"Come in," he said, looking from her to Hudson.

"I can wait here," Hudson offered, but she reached for his hand, linking their fingers. No way could she do this without him.

Crossing the threshold was like stepping into a time capsule. Her father still had the same brown plaid sofa with twin brown recliners flanking either side, all positioned to take advantage of the TV screen. The back to the TV had disappeared and he'd mounted a flat screen to the wall, adding a console table underneath. Those were the only real improvements. She glanced at the contents, half expecting to see a VHS machine, but she found a Blu-ray player instead.

Her father looked exactly the same as he had

as far back as Madelyn could remember. He had a slightly round stomach from too much sitting and a sunburn showing at his V-neck shirt despite owning a clock repair shop and spending much of his time indoors. His light brown hair was graying at the temples. He wasn't wealthy by any stretch of the imagination but they'd had enough to cover the basics. He was the kind of guy who could fix just about anything. But he'd shown no interest in repairing what most needed to be mended in his home—his relationship with his daughter. The irony of that sat heavy in Madelyn's thoughts. He'd spent days off tinkering in the garage, not coming in until supper. He'd park in front of the screen with a TV tray.

Most of the time, Madelyn had read while she ate at the table. Alone.

"I know she was already pregnant when you married her." Madelyn came right out with it, unable to skirt the issues any longer. "The question is, did you?"

"Do you want a cup of coffee?" her father said, avoiding looking directly at her. Instead he looked at Hudson, who introduced himself.

She didn't really want to waste time but there was something about her father's expression that caused her to think he needed a minute. It was that same look sources got when they were about to tell her something that was difficult for them to say. "Okay."

He disappeared into the kitchen as Madelyn showed Hudson to the round table and chairs near the sliding glass patio door. He scooted his chair next to hers so that the outsides of their thighs touched. There was something so reassuring about his touch.

Charles brought over two full cups, hers and the special one meant for guests. He disappeared into the galley-style kitchen before returning with his #1 Dad mug. She'd saved money she'd earned from chores and received in birthday presents to afford it and remembered being so proud when he opened it that Father's Day when she was eight years old. He'd given her a kiss on the forehead despite his distant expression and then used it every day from then on, as far as she knew.

Her father took a sip of the fresh brew before slowly exhaling, studying the rim of his cup intently. It took everything inside her not to barrage him with the dozens of questions flooding her. But being there in her family home, the one she'd shared with him, brought an onslaught of tender memories. On the table was her baby photo album, the one he'd meticulously put together and given her when she turned eighteen.

There were so many questions swirling. Madelyn pulled on a well of patience she didn't know existed until now. Something in her had changed and she felt a sense of compassion instead of anger for the man who couldn't seem to find the right words to tell her that he wasn't her father.

"I loved her," he finally said before compressing his lips like he had to clamp his mouth shut in order to keep hold of his emotions. "She'd left me because she wanted to go to the city. Said she'd die of boredom if she stayed in Halifax Trail, where we're from."

He paused long enough to take another sip of coffee, white-knuckling the mug.

"I always blamed myself because I refused when she asked me to go with her." He looked up at Madelyn but quickly refocused on the rim. "I was stubborn back then."

A wave of compassion washed over Madelyn. Being here with her father made her remember all those times she'd climbed in his lap while he read the morning paper. He'd bounce her on his knee.

"Told her my life was in Halifax Trail and the

city had nothing to offer me," he said. "Looking back, she took that to mean I didn't love her. That wasn't the case at all. But she didn't know how much it broke my heart that she could walk away so easily. I've never been one to show my emotions." His voice hitched.

"Did she lie to you and say the baby was yours when she came back?" Madelyn asked. For some reason the answer mattered very much to her.

"No, she didn't," he quickly countered. "I knew the whole story. She'd gotten herself in trouble with a married man. She needed a place to hide. I knew that her father would disown her if she turned up pregnant and alone, so I asked her to marry me. Told her I didn't have much and my life was here but she could have everything I owned."

Madelyn pushed off the table and got to her feet. He knew. Her stomach tightened. So, he'd loved her mother but not her.

"When I lost her, I felt like the world had ended," he said. "I'd been the one to insist on paying for everything even though—" he didn't look at Madelyn this time "—*he* said he'd cover her medical bills."

Anger rose from Madelyn's chest, licking her veins with white-hot embers. "Is that why you pushed me away? Because I reminded you of *him*?"

"What?" Her father seemed genuinely surprised at her outburst.

"Don't look at me like you don't know what I'm talking about. We both know you were forced to take care of me after Mom died." She paced. The urge to open the door, run outside and keep going until she dropped from exhaustion burned inside her chest.

"You were the best thing that came out of a bad situation," he said with a bewildered look on his face.

"Do you expect me to believe that?" she shot

back. "Or is that how you show love to people? Always keeping them at arm's length?"

A few tears streaked his cheeks as he sat there, soberly.

"I had no idea you took it that way," he finally said. "You were so much like your mom when you were little that I figured one of these days you'd walk out, too." His voice broke on the last couple of words. "I've been preparing myself for the day I'd lose you, too, because you were always smart and full of life. Just like her."

The force of those words was a cannon to her chest. She stopped, trying to process the implications of what he'd said. He'd been afraid she'd be the one to leave?

Madelyn whirled around to face her father.

"I've always lived in fear that you would figure out that I wasn't your *real* dad and you'd push me away." He wouldn't look anywhere but at the coffee mug in his hand, staring at it as if he was enthralled, as more tears streaked down his cheeks. "It wasn't a matter of *if* but *when*."

She took in a few deep breaths, praying for the right words. His anguish was evident on his worn face and he looked so old to her then. Fragile. The strong man who'd seemed so impenetrable looked like he might shatter. But the only thing that splintered was Madelyn's anger. She'd never seen her father look so vulnerable and her heart caved.

She started toward him as tears burned her eyes. He met her in the middle of the room. "I'll always love you. Nothing will ever change that. And I need you to start meeting me halfway or our relationship won't work. When I call, I need you to pick up the phone because no matter what a piece of paper says you'll always be my father. And I need you now more than ever."

Her father pulled her into a bear hug. "Forgive an old fool if I promise to do better? I don't want to lose you."

Madelyn embraced her father in the warmest hug she'd ever known.

"I'll admit that I've always feared this day would come, but having everything out in the open is actually a relief." He wiped the tears away. "I couldn't have loved you more than if you'd been my own blood."

"You're my family, Dad."

"Can you forgive me?"

"Absolutely, and I should've talked to you about this sooner." Looking back, she could see how he was the kind of person who had a hard time showing his feelings and she wished they'd cleared the air long ago. She'd confused his fear with a lack of love for her. Now that she realized he'd tried to stay aloof because he was afraid that she'd reject him when she learned of her heritage, she could forgive him. "Even if I had known Mike Butler was my father when he was still alive, you were the one who put on an apron and baked a cake for every birthday I can remember, not him."

"He offered," he defended. "We kept you from him and I never did feel that was right for either one of you. He could've given you things and you deserve to have the world."

"Did you know that I left town because his lawyer contacted me?" she asked.

He shook his head.

"All these years, Maverick Mike kept quiet." It was all she had to say.

"From what I've heard, he wasn't a bad man underneath all the flash and show," her father said, wiping away another stray tear.

"If I'm good, it's because of you. Blood isn't important. Being there every day for a child is." She embraced her father, remembering the look on his face when he'd dropped her off the first day of kindergarten. He must not've realized she was watching him out the window but it was the first time she remembered seeing him get emotional. "Now that everything's in the open there's no more need to be afraid."

"I was stupid." Charles hugged her tighter and for a second she was his little girl again, being comforted by her father's arms. There was only one other time when she'd felt safe and that was in Hudson's arms. But then, he was practically a stranger.

"I love you, Maddie-cake." He hadn't called her that since she was eight years old.

"I love you, too, Dad."

The two reclaimed their seats when the hugs and tears seemed to be over.

"Owen hasn't stopped by, has he?" Madelyn asked.

"Haven't seen him," her dad said with a glance toward Hudson.

She smiled through the awkward moment.

"Steer clear of him for the next couple of

weeks. We broke up and he hasn't been taking it well," she said.

"I figured as much." Another quick glance toward Hudson.

"He's a friend." There was no way she was going to try to explain what neither she nor Hudson had attempted to define.

When the coffee cups were drained, it was time to head back to the ranch. They said their goodbyes with promises to be better about staying in touch.

"It was a pleasure meeting you," Hudson said, shaking her father's hand.

Madelyn's moment of happiness was derailed when she saw the back bumper of a white sedan cut a close corner at the end of the street.

"We have to go. *Now.*"

Chapter Sixteen

"Any sign of the white sedan?" Madelyn asked as she checked the side-view mirror.

"Nothing from my view, but just because I can't see it doesn't mean it's not back there somewhere," Hudson warned. "It might not be the one we're looking for anyway."

Madelyn had had the same thought as she double-checked the road. There were a few cars and sport-utility vehicles, none of which were white.

"Your father seems like a good man," Hudson said. "He'll have a hard time forgiving himself."

"Anyone who would take someone else's child and never say one way or the other gets extra points in my book," she pointed out.

"I don't think he saw it like that at all," he said.

"Oh, yeah? How so?"

"Seems to me that you always belonged to him in his heart."

She wondered if Hudson would ever forgive himself for his past. Being with her father brought home a different point. One that she didn't want to apply to her current situation but couldn't stop the comparison. People only changed when they wanted to.

"I'm still touched by your acceptance of him, flaws and all," he stated.

"Perfection is an impossible goal. Love and forgiveness matter so much more." Her cell buzzed and she retrieved it from her handbag. It was a text from Harlan that read, He used to be a cop in Houston. Blood on his hands. Want to know more? Call me ASAP.

"What is it?" Hudson's voice broke through her heavy thoughts. He'd lied to her. He'd been lying to her all along.

"Were you going to tell me that you worked for Houston PD?"

Hudson didn't say a word but she could feel the tension fill the cabin like a thick fog. The rest of the drive was dead silent.

"My past is none of your business," Hudson mumbled, parking the truck in his garage. "And you had no right poking around in my background without my permission."

"Maybe you should've disclosed that before we slept together, Hudson." She hopped out of the truck and slammed the door.

Hudson practically flew around the vehicle. He captured her wrist in his hand and she ignored those infuriating frissons of electricity coursing through her.

"Don't leave. Not like this," he said.

"I can't stick around here anymore and we both know it. Not if you won't tell me anything about you."

"What does it matter? Will it change the way you feel about me?" he asked. He had that same look as her father, the one where he didn't seem to have the right words—only Hudson wasn't trying to find them.

"I'm going to the Butlers'. I can call them once I get my stuff together. I'm sure the sheriff will speak to Trent and Kelsey and get back to me." She jerked out of his grip and stalked inside to the guest room. Her bag was open and her stuff flung everywhere. Anger roared through her.

He stood in the hallway, his arms crossed as he leaned against the doorjamb.

"What's happening?" he asked.

"You tell me," she fired back.

"I'm not the one packing," he said.

"You want to know what's really going on?" She froze, thought twice about saying the words on the tip of her tongue. It had been an exhausting day already and all she wanted to do was tumble into bed in his arms and sleep. But then what?

"That's what I said."

"I'm falling for you, Hudson Dale, and that's ridiculous even to me because I don't even know who you really are. How stupid is that? I don't know anything about your past or who you are, and you have no plans to tell me, either," she said. "Your life is a mystery and I'm not supposed to ask questions. I'm just supposed to accept everything at face value and it seems to me that if you won't let me in there's nothing I can do about it. And the worst part is that I know you have feelings for me but you'll never let anything develop between us."

"What you said about your father made an impact on me," he began, and she sat on the bed with her back facing him. She didn't want him to see her so close to losing it right then. Tears already streaked her cheeks and her emotions felt wrung out from her earlier encounter with her father. At least that had had a positive outcome.

"There isn't much that can't be forgiven once people start communicating," she said.

She heard him take a step toward her but he must've stopped because all fell quiet again.

"Not everything can," he said before she heard him turn around and walk out of the room.

Whatever he'd done before seemed like it would haunt him forever. She grabbed the handbag she'd tossed onto the floor and made the call to Ed Staples.

There were two problems with staying at Hudson's ranch. One, someone had figured out where she was, and that couldn't be good. And two, sticking around threatened to destroy her when this was all over and it was time to go home.

She'd made a huge error in judgment in dating Owen and she liked to think she learned from her mistakes. Comparing the two seemed absurd to her, even while her emotions were all over the place, but she'd gone into a relationship with Owen blindly, ignoring all the early warning signs of him being a little too possessive.

She'd give him one thing: he'd seemed like an open book, telling her everything about him and his family from day one. Not that it mattered because she and Hudson would never have a chance at a real relationship until he forgave himself.

"Is the offer of a roof over my head still available?" she asked Ed Staples when he picked up on the first ring.

"It is," he said.

"Then I'd like to take the Butler family up

on their generosity. I can be there in less than half an hour," she stated.

"I'll alert the guard at the front gate," he said and sounded happier than she'd expected. Maybe he liked the idea of righting a wrong for his friend.

"Perfect." She gathered the last of her things, shoved them inside her overnight bag and wiped away a few stray tears before stalking into the living room in search of her car keys.

Hudson was in the kitchen, leaning against the granite counter with a mug of coffee in his hand. "Ready?"

She glanced around on the countertop. "As soon as I find my keys I'll be out of your hair."

"You mean these?" He pulled a set from out of his pocket and twirled them around the finger of his free hand.

She made a move toward him but he captured them in his palm, took a big sip of coffee and started toward the garage.

"What are you doing?" she asked.

"Coming with you." He cracked an infuriating smile.

"I didn't invite you."

"Yes, you did. At the Butlers' house and, besides, you made a good point." His intense brown eyes drew her in.

"And what was that?"

"It's not safe here anymore," he said. "We'll stay at the Butlers' until I can secure the ranch."

"What about Bullseye and the other horses?" she asked, her heart betraying her with a little flip at the thought of him coming with her.

"Let me worry about them." He opened the door.

"Are you sure this is a good idea?"

His strong facade broke for an instant and he looked tired. "I don't know what's going on between us. Or maybe I'm not that stupid and I do. I'm not ready to put words to what we have but you in my bed is the first time I've slept in longer than I can remember and I don't want you to go. It's not safe here and I get that, so I'm coming with you."

"I don't need you there. I'll have plenty of security," she said.

"True, but will you have this?" He ate up the real estate between them in two strides, placed his hand on her hip and pulled her toward him until their lips fused together. The earth shifted underneath her feet as a flame engulfed her in two seconds flat, catching her off guard.

She was breathless by the time he pulled back and she could see that he was, too.

"It's the damnedest thing, isn't it?" His face broke into a brilliant show of straight white teeth.

Madelyn couldn't help herself. She smiled, too.

He held out his hand. "Ready?"

The battle between what her heart wanted and her mind warned against raged. She took in a sharp breath. "We're back at ground zero. You haven't told me anything about your past and I still don't know who you are."

"I will," he said with earnest eyes. "All I need to know is if that's good enough for now."

Tentatively, she took the hand he was offering. All logic said she should make him give her something more.

Her heart took over as he pressed a kiss to her lips. This time, the brush was so gentle and yet lit so many fires inside her.

And she was powerless against it. She hoped that didn't come back and burn her.

PULLING INTO THE Butler estate, Madelyn immediately noticed a deputy's SUV parked out front and her heart sank.

"I wonder what that's about." Her first thought was that something else had happened on the ranch and she immediately second-guessed her decision to come. Was anywhere safe anymore?

"Let's find out." Hudson parked and they walked to the front door hand in hand.

It took a couple of minutes for someone to answer. It was Ella Butler and the look on her face dropped Madelyn's heart to her toes.

"Come in." Ella ushered them inside.

Madelyn followed Ella into the same dining room they'd been in yesterday.

Ed Staples immediately stepped forward. "You're going to hear something disturbing, but I assure you no one here knows what's happening."

Madelyn noticed that Hudson had positioned himself between her and the rest of the Butlers. Everyone was standing and Deputy Harley nodded toward her.

"What is it? What's going on?" Madelyn asked.

The deputy angled his body in her direction. "We found traces of lipstick markings on the bathroom mirror where you said someone had written a note. Forensics returned the sample and we were able to identify a brand. It's an expensive lipstick, not something many folks around here would know about or be able to afford. So, the sheriff thought it might be a good idea to come here and ask if anyone knew anything about Rat-tat Red."

He looked to her.

"Never heard of it in my life," she said.

"Neither had any of us, but then we discovered the brand is from Paris and there's only one family in town who would have the kind of money to buy Rat-tat Red lipstick in France, so we stopped by to inquire if there'd been a burglary," he continued.

"And we said that there hasn't been one that we know of." Ella was wringing her hands together.

The deputy agreed with her admission. "And that presents a problem for us because when we looked in Cadence Butler's cosmetic drawer, you can guess what we found."

"Rat-tat Red," Madelyn said.

"That's right. So, if there wasn't a burglary, that means someone with access to her cosmetics wrote that on your mirror." The deputy stood, feet apart, in an athletic stance.

"My sister wasn't even here. She's sick and she's been gone." And then it seemed to dawn on Ella. "When did this happen?"

"Three days ago between the hours of 3:00 and 5:00 p.m.," the deputy responded.

Ella sat down at the table, looking a little lost. "She was here during that window but there's no way she would…"

"Do you know Trent Buford?" Madelyn asked.

Ella's forehead scrunched. "No."

"Your sister might," Madelyn said, looking to Hudson. He nodded. "Seems convenient that Cadence left when she did."

Hudson clasped his hands. "She would

have to be working with someone else to pull this off."

"He works at the motel. Doesn't seem like they'd run in the same circles," Madelyn said.

"They could be linked by Kelsey," he said.

Ella grunted. "That name sounds familiar."

"Where is Cadence now?" the deputy asked Ella. "I'll need to speak to her in order to establish a connection."

Madelyn looked at everyone differently now. The few tentative strands of trust had snapped the minute the lipstick was traced to this house.

"I'm not sure," Ella admitted, "but I can call her." She was already looking for her cell.

Dade leaned forward and rested his elbows on his knees. "Looking at this from your perspective, I can see how damaging this seems. We aren't the kind of people who would do something like this. No one is more upset than we are to find this out, and I'm certain my sister isn't involved."

"We'll get to the bottom of this," Dalton agreed.

Madelyn would reserve judgment for the time being. The twins seemed sincere and Ella appeared distraught.

"She's not picking up," Ella said, ending the call. She made a face as she fired off a text. "I just can't imagine that she would be involved in something like this."

"Who else has access to the bedrooms?" the deputy asked.

"May, our housekeeper, but I'd trust her with my life," Ella said, and the twins were nodding.

"We limit people from coming and going ever since our dad was killed and Ella was targeted," Dade said.

Which narrowed down the suspect list to the people in the room and the missing sister.

Madelyn turned to Hudson. "Let's go."

"Don't," Ella pleaded. "At least not until we can clear this up. This is crazy and I don't want you to leave thinking that we're some lunatic family. We're actually pretty decent people, and although we haven't been the most welcoming, we want you to know that we'll adjust. Whether you turn out to be our sister or not, our father wanted you to be part of this family, and we haven't been good at respecting his wishes."

"I'd hate for any of you to put yourself out," Madelyn shot back, leading with her emotions. She reminded herself that staying objective was how a good reporter uncovered the truth. Living that axiom was so much harder when it came to her life.

"What she means is that we're actually a nice bunch who look out for each other," Dade interjected. "Our relationship with our father was complicated."

Ed stepped in front of the French doors.

"I was hoping to do this with the entire family in the room, but since that seems impossible with—" he glanced at the deputy "—the current…*situation*, I think this might be as good a time as we'll get. The DNA test results came back."

Chapter Seventeen

"And?" Madelyn didn't want to admit how much she needed the confirmation. She already had proof from Charles. He'd told her that she wasn't his and yet her logical mind needed this evidence. Her hand came up to her dragonfly necklace, fingering the details.

"You're a Butler, Madelyn."

There was something primal about needing to know something so basic, something that most people took for granted, which was where they came from. Knowing who her parents were.

"And as I was going through more of your

father's things this afternoon, I found this." He handed over another envelope.

She stared at it like it was a bomb, remembering how much her life had changed when he'd done this before.

"It won't bite. I promise," Ed said softly, urging her to take the offering.

She did and she pulled out the first item, a picture of her about to dive into the water. She remembered that city meet like it was yesterday. "This was senior year. I won that race with a record-setting time. But who took this?"

"I didn't," Ed said. "I believe it was your father."

She dumped a few similar pictures out onto her hand and it was like taking a trip back into the past. Photos of various swim meets, most likely taken with a telephoto lens. There were papers, too. Letters from coaches at various top colleges.

"He's the one who made sure I got into a

good college, isn't he?" she asked Ed. "It all makes sense now. And being inducted into the school's hall of fame. The donation didn't come from alumni. It was him."

"Seems like he was very proud of your accomplishments, Miss Kensington." Ed had that same fatherly pride she'd heard in her own father's voice when she'd told him about the ceremony.

A hot tear streaked her cheek.

"Sounds about right," Dade muttered under his breath, and it seemed Charles wasn't the only father who wasn't stellar about sharing emotions.

Madelyn turned her back to everyone and studied the contents of the envelope, not wanting anyone to see just how sensitive she was. There were pictures of her over the years and something she treasured even more, photos of her mother.

Hudson moved behind her and brought his

hands to her shoulders, bringing warmth to her tense muscles. It caught her off guard that Mike Butler being proud of her made her emotional.

Had Cadence Butler discovered this? Been jealous? It was convenient timing that she had the flu and was out of town. Had she set all this up to spook Madelyn? To get her out of the way?

Or was someone else trying to protect the family?

So much more made sense about her swimming scholarship that had landed almost out of the blue. Even her coach had seemed surprised and she'd known that he'd been holding something back when he'd delivered the news. Mike, her father—and that still seemed too weird to acknowledge—had obviously set everything up. If his right-hand person, Ed Staples, didn't know about it then he must've done it himself, and that meant more to her than she should allow.

"I think we should go," she said, feeling suddenly awkward in the house, tucking the envelope along with its contents into her purse.

"Please, stay for a little while. At least until we hear back from my sister," Ella said, motioning toward the dining chair.

Madelyn wanted answers. Staying, spending time with the Butlers would give her a chance to get to know them better. And there was another pull to the ranch that she wasn't ready to analyze but it made her feel closer to her mother.

Half an hour later, Ella's phone rang. She glanced at the screen. "It's my sister."

The deputy had already left to continue his investigation elsewhere, promising to follow up on all leads. He'd also asked to be notified when Cadence checked in and said he'd be trying to find her on his own. Everyone was clear that she needed to report to the sheriff's office immediately.

"Where are you?" Ella immediately asked.

"Put the call on speaker," Dade said, no room for argument in his tone. Did he suspect his baby sister of foul play?

"Oh, right, sorry," Ella said. She moved the cell away from her ear and did as he'd asked.

"What's going on, Cadence?" Dade asked with authority. He would've made a great law-enforcement officer.

"Nothing," she said, and there was more than a hint of defensiveness in her tone.

"Don't mess around. This is serious." Impatience edged his tone. "If you did something to Madelyn Kensington you need to speak up because the sheriff's office is involved and there are real consequences."

"What are you talking about? You're going to have to fill me in because I have no idea," Cadence said with a shaky voice that quickly recovered.

"Tell us what you know about Madelyn." He

glanced up at her and she didn't know him well enough to figure out what he was thinking.

"I have no idea who that is," Cadence said, but the tremble to her voice said otherwise. Or maybe she really was still sick like they'd said before. She definitely sounded off to Madelyn. But then, maybe she was just reading too much into the situation. It was impossible to stay objective when she was *this* close to the story.

"Sounds like you might," Dade said, and she appreciated his honesty and directness. He certainly wasn't pulling any punches now even though he'd defended his sister fervently before new evidence came to light. "Like I said before, if you know anything about what's going on with Madelyn Kensington—" she noticed he stopped short of calling her their sister, but then she realized that he might be trying to trip Cadence up "—you need to speak up now or face the very real possibility of spending time in jail. Dad isn't here to bail you out this time."

His words were harsh and his stare intent. Even Ella seemed to feel like he'd gone too far when she shot him a look.

Madelyn looked to Hudson, who stood strong and silent beside her. He stared at the travertine floor intently, expectantly. She thought about his background, his former employment with Houston PD. From what she could see so far, he would've been great at his job. Missing the action was most likely the reason he'd been so eager to help before. Don't get her wrong, ranching life seemed to suit him, but the pace was much slower and there were no adrenaline rushes. Most of the cops she'd known needed them in order to feel alive.

"I already said I don't know her," Cadence said, but there was real fear in her voice now.

"Cadence, who's Trent?"

The line went dead quiet.

"You should come home," Ella said. "Now."

"I'll be on the next flight," she said.

"How long will that take?" Ella asked.

"Hold on." The sounds of fingers on a laptop came through. "I can be home tonight."

"That's too late," Dade said. "We'll send a pilot to pick you up now."

Cadence issued a harsh sigh. "I'm at the lake house in Boulder Mountain. There are fires, so the private airstrip is closed."

Dade didn't seem impressed with the news. "I'll arrange for an earlier flight out of Denver airport. Can you get there within the hour?"

"That should work." She sounded resigned.

"We'll see you this afternoon," he said.

Ella ended the call.

Hudson's hand was on Madelyn's elbow now as he squeezed. She guessed that he had something to say that he didn't want the others to hear.

"Okay if we take a walk?" Madelyn asked, looking to the concerned eldest Butler.

"Of course," Ella said.

Madelyn walked out with Hudson close on her heels. Whatever he needed to say seemed urgent.

HUDSON FELT LIKE he had a pretty good read on the twins and Ella. All three of them were innocent.

"I don't trust Cadence," he said to Madelyn after making sure they'd walked out of earshot. He glanced behind them, checking to ensure no one had followed. Until they had definitive proof none of the Butlers were involved, they needed to watch their backs. "She's either hiding or covering."

"I got the same impression but I'm curious what makes you think that," Madelyn said, eyeing him carefully.

He hadn't given her much to go on or trust him and she'd shown that she was willing to give him leeway. Thinking about the past, let alone talking about it, had been something he'd been avoiding. Normally, when he thought about it a heavy curtain dropped around his shoulders.

This time was different.

"You already know that I used to be a cop in Houston," he admitted and discovered it wasn't horrible to talk about.

"Most cops I've met would never leave the job." She folded her arms like she was readying herself for the wall that would come up between them. She was a quick learner and he regretted the times he'd done that when he should've forged ahead into uncomfortable territory and talked. "What made you?"

A mix of emotion swirled through Hudson, bubbling to the surface. Talking could make everything a whole lot worse, although his situation—he hadn't really been able to sleep until this beauty had come into his life—didn't seem like it could get much worse.

He could try to reason himself to death or he

could go on instinct and tell her what had happened. "My partner was killed."

"And you blame yourself?" she asked.

"The bullet was meant for me," he supplied, waiting for the heavy downpour of emotions that always came when he thought about it, let alone tried to discuss it.

"And he—"

"She," he corrected, and it seemed to immediately dawn on her that the two had been having an affair. "Was pregnant."

"Oh" was all she said at first. She wrapped her arms around his neck, placed her head on his chest and said in barely a whisper, "I'm so sorry, Hudson."

Those words were all she had to say to lighten the war raging inside him because she turned to him when she spoke and that one look she gave shattered another layer of his defenses. There were so few walls left between her and the real him and he felt exposed.

He looped his arms around her waist, aware that another layer was disintegrating. He thought about how helpless he'd been to help Misty and he was in the same boat with Madelyn now, too.

The thought of not being able to protect Madelyn, of the possibility of losing her, too, hit like a physical punch with lightning speed. He glanced around, thinking that someone on this ranch could be threatening her. His own judgment was swayed by his closeness to the case. A good cop never went in alone, like he'd tried to do on the shift with Misty. He was trying to protect her and all he'd really done was end up getting her killed. He'd stopped treating her like a partner and had started looking at her as the woman carrying his child. It had cost him a whole helluva lot. It didn't seem to matter then or now that she hadn't been 100 percent sure the baby was even his. She'd admitted that to him on their dinner break. She'd started seeing someone else when she thought she might be getting too close to Hudson.

Hudson had learned from his mistakes and he wouldn't try to do any of this alone. He and Madelyn needed to involve as many people as possible. They needed to work with law enforcement, the Butlers and anyone else who wanted to be involved in order to ensure her safety.

"You have to go home," he said. "We'll talk to the police in your area and bring them up to date. They're already aware of the restraining order and I'll call my old boss and see if I can plead your case. He'll believe the threat is real, when I explain to him what's going on. You're not safe here. The sheriff is too overloaded. I can't do this on my own and I can't allow anything to happen to you."

This close, he could breathe in the scent of her shampoo, which smelled of citrus and spring.

"I want to see Cadence first. I want to look

her in the eyes so I can tell if she's lying." Madelyn didn't budge. She stood there with a fixed, determined look.

"The threat won't stop if it's coming from inside the Butler camp. They stand to gain millions if you don't exist," he said. "I didn't consider them a serious possibility until today."

"If it's not her, someone also targeted Ella. What if more than one person was involved?" she asked.

"A good investigator follows the evidence and right now that leads to Cadence Butler," he said. "She has motive and had opportunity."

"What about the incident at your place earlier?" she asked. "That couldn't have been her."

"Let me think on this some more." He frowned because she was right. She was also overlooking the possibility that now hit him like a truck. There could be multiple issues at work, converging. The first was her ex. The incident at his ranch and then at her father's house earlier had more of a stalker ring to it. How did Trent fit into the picture? A male figure hiding in the woods, watching. That could be Owen or someone hired by him. This all circled back to the road-rage incident and the white sedan.

Nothing made sense, nothing clicked.

More than anything, Hudson wanted to give Madelyn her life back. Maybe it was selfish but he needed to know that she'd be all right. The feeling in the pit of his gut warned him. And he needed to distance himself from her.

Chapter Eighteen

Hudson stayed within arm's reach for the rest of the afternoon, but he made no physical contact with Madelyn. There was something different about him that she couldn't quite put her finger on. His stance was aggressive and she figured he was going into investigator mode.

Madelyn kept an emotional distance.

At least he'd shared part of his history with her. The constant guilt he seemed to carry made more sense now that she knew, but there was precious little she could do about it.

Dade walked outside and signaled. "Cadence was picked up by the deputy at the airport.

She's being taken to the sheriff's office and should be there in fifteen minutes."

"We'll meet you there," Hudson said with a look toward Madelyn. She grabbed her purse and they bolted to his truck.

Twenty minutes later, they were parking at the sheriff's office. Media swarmed the Butler vehicles and Madelyn had the very sobering realization that would be happening to her as soon as news of her paternity got out. There'd be a feeding frenzy when word got out that Maverick Mike's illegitimate child had surfaced. This was her chosen career and she'd always believed in being transparent, in telling the truth. So, why did it feel like the walls were closing in on her?

Because it was her life, dammit, and her professional values just clashed with it. As a journalist, she felt people had the right to know. As a person, she didn't want her life splashed across the news. She shelved those heavy thoughts, kept her head down and walked inside. That would be her life soon enough, but for now she had a little anonymity and she intended to hold on to it until the very last second.

It occurred to her that Hudson's life would be tabloid fodder, as well. His association with her would ensure it. He'd lost a partner, a future wife and a child in the time it took for a bullet to split the air. He'd gone to great lengths to keep his life private. He'd quit his job and relocated to a small town. There was no way he wanted people digging around in his background, and now that she'd be news, it was something she had to consider in order to protect him. He had to come first. She couldn't imagine that he'd be willing to subject himself to media scrutiny for a relationship neither of them was clear about anyway.

None of that mattered now. Madelyn needed to get to the bottom of who was targeting her.

And with Cadence already in the sheriff's office, she figured it wouldn't be long before the truth came out. She absently fingered the dragonfly necklace.

Hudson was already making a beeline toward Doris. "Can we watch?"

The older woman grunted. "And get me fired?"

"We both know this office would fall apart without you," he said.

Doris's face flamed. "Are you flirting with me again, Hudson Dale?"

He chuckled that low rumble from his chest that she'd found so sexy. "Guess I am. Is it working?"

Now it was Doris's turn to laugh. "A little bit."

"Then I'm not trying hard enough." He nodded toward the hallway.

Another frustrated sound tore from her throat. "Go ahead. I can always eat cat food if I run out of money once I lose my job."

"You know I'd never let that happen." Hudson motioned toward the hallway but he didn't reach for Madelyn's hand this time.

She followed him to a small room. Next door was an interview room. A two-way mirror allowed her to see clearly and she could listen to the interview through a speaker. Deputy Harley was there, sitting across the table from Cadence. She was petite and her face was very pale. She was hunkered forward, clutching her stomach, and there was a trash can at her feet. Didn't someone say she had the flu?

Based on her looks, it was easy to see that she was a Butler and Madelyn recognized her from the family portrait hanging in the dining room. Madelyn remembered that in the picture, everyone wore jeans and white shirts. They looked to be out on the front lawn. Maverick Mike was in the center and his children flanked his sides. They were younger, maybe early teens, and their father wore a collared shirt along with a white Stetson. From what she could tell, not everyone who smiled in the picture was happy. Obviously, looks could be deceiving. How well she knew that, she mused, thinking back to Owen. This would all be over soon enough and she'd return home to deal with him. The strange feeling in the pit of her stomach surprisingly had little to do with facing Owen and so much more to do with the handsome cowboy she'd grown to care about. Love?

"You said before that you have no idea who might've written the note on the mirror of room twenty-six at the Red Rope Inn," the deputy said, leaning forward like he had to strain to hear Cadence. He was in her face, encroaching on her physical space, a tactic Madelyn had seen used dozens of times in interviews.

"That's right," Cadence responded, but her voice was shaky. The voice, the eyes revealed so much about a person. She was lying.

"Are you sure about that, Ms. Butler, because

we're going to subpoena your cell phone records," he continued.

Cadence started working the napkin in her hands and her gaze flew to the floor.

"You'd be surprised the trail people leave behind when they do something wrong. Especially good people who don't normally cross a line like this," he said, dropping his tone to conspiratorial.

"I don't know what you're talking about," she responded, and when Madelyn looked closely, she realized a few tears were streaming down her cheeks. "I'm sorry. I'm tired and not feeling well."

"Where's the white sedan?" the deputy pressed.

Cadence's body language immediately changed. "What?"

"The vehicle you used to run Ms. Kensington off the road," he continued.

"I don't know anything about that." Her head shook furiously and then a look of panic crossed her features. "Is she okay? Because you already know what my sister's been through."

"How do you know Trent?" he asked.

She froze.

"She didn't do it," Hudson said so low Madelyn almost didn't hear it. She was thinking the same thing and he confirmed her thoughts.

The deputy came at the question from a couple of angles and netted the same response. Cadence had no idea about the sedan. Just as Madelyn started to write the whole interview off as useless, Cadence's shoulders rocked and tears flowed.

"You were here long enough to write the threatening note, weren't you?" the deputy said, focusing in on the area he could make progress on.

"I was," she said. More tears flowed. "I don't know anything about a white sedan or anyone trying to run her off the road but I wrote the message on her mirror."

The deputy leaned back, folded his arms and said, "Tell me exactly how you did it."

Cadence blew her nose into the napkin and bent forward like she was about to retch. She took a sip of the water that had been provided before making eye contact with the deputy.

"I did it to protect my family. All I was trying to do was scare her, though," Cadence quickly added. "I would never hurt anyone or put them in any danger."

"How'd you get into the motel room?" he asked.

"Trent was a year below me in school," she said. "I flirted with him a little bit to get the key and swore him to secrecy."

So, Trent was guilty.

"Then I panicked about the whole episode but it was already too late to go back and fix it. Trent freaked out worse than I did and left work early," she said.

"I have no doubt your cell records will let us know if you're lying."

She pulled her cell from her purse, punched in a few numbers that were most likely meant to unlock the screen and pushed it toward him on the table. "See for yourself. I've told you everything I know. I feel like the biggest jerk for making someone else afraid. It was impulsive and I had no idea that there was a real threat out there. The worst part is that I heard about what my sister went through and I feel awful now for putting someone else through that."

At least they knew how Trent fit into the picture. But what would happen to him now?

"How long have you known Kelsey?" The deputy glanced up from scrolling through her phone. He'd been looking at something intensely and Madelyn figured it was either her call log or text history.

Cadence stared at the wall like she was drawing a blank. "I can't help you there since I don't know a Kelsey."

"You sure about that?" the deputy asked.

Cadence made eyes at the deputy. "I think I'd know if she was familiar."

"Then you don't know that she's suing Ms. Kensington," he stated.

"No, but news she's a Butler must've leaked to someone and I'm guessing maybe that person was Trent," Cadence said.

"Interesting."

"What's going to happen to him?" Cadence asked. "This is all my fault. Not his. I'd feel terrible if he was brought up on charges."

"We'll let you know when he surfaces," the deputy said.

"Where is he?" she asked.

The deputy shrugged his shoulders.

"Can I call him?" she asked.

"Tell him to come in. He's either a witness or a suspect. If he turns himself in, he's looking at a few hours of community service with a stern warning. If not, he moves to the suspect list. How he handles himself in the next couple of days determines his fate." The deputy folded his hands and put them on the table.

"He'll be in. I'll make sure," Cadence promised.

More questions swirled in Madelyn's mind. She couldn't go back to the Butler ranch, not with Cadence home. If the youngest Butler wasn't connected to the white sedan then someone still had it out for her.

"IT'S BEEN A long day and I'm tired," Madelyn said, rubbing the spot between her eyes as a headache formed. "I'm ready to go."

Hudson took her by the hand and led her out of the sheriff's office. She ignored the way his strong, warm hand made her heart leap.

He opened the door for her first before walking around and sitting in the driver's seat. He'd excused himself earlier and set everything up with his old boss. Doris had had a friend pick up Madelyn's bag.

The plan was for Hudson to take her home and yet the word seemed so foreign now. Her place had felt comfortable before. She'd always believed that once she knew her mother and improved her relationship with her father she'd finally feel at peace. All the pieces of Madelyn's past had finally been fit together for her, and yet she'd never felt more distance between who she thought she was and who she truly was. That probably didn't even make sense, she thought.

A couple of ibuprofen and a warm shower should make her feel human again. At least she hoped it would.

Being away from Cattle Barge was also supposed to ease the threat. After all, everything had started the minute she'd driven into town. Her apartment should be okay.

But would she ever really feel safe again?

Lack of sleep and the threatening headache had her not thinking straight as she watched the road ahead. Of course she would feel safe. Once her life was back on track and she could put this nightmare behind her.

Hudson was quiet on the ride home. He'd driven her convertible with a plan to return to his ranch in Cattle Barge using a car service. It was long past nightfall by the time they reached her place but it was impossible to miss the activity in the parking lot. There were reporters everywhere. News was out.

Madelyn lived on the second floor because it was safer. She almost laughed out loud. Nothing felt safe anymore.

Hudson circled the block instead of parking. "We could go to a hotel."

"Would that make it harder to protect me?" She'd picked up on the hesitation in his voice.

He parked, took her hand and shielded her

from the slew of media rushing toward her. It didn't take long to sweep the place.

"It's okay," he said. He held up the key to her convertible. "You'll be safe while I'm gone. I'll be back as soon as I call on my old boss."

With all these reporters, at least Madelyn would get a break from Owen. There were too many witnesses.

Madelyn glanced around. It was comforting that her couch was in the same spot. There were two chairs positioned around the rug for easy conversation. She'd decorated the place two years ago thinking about all the entertaining she planned to do. When in reality, all she did was work and sleep there. She'd promised herself that she'd get a dog to make the place feel more like home. But all she'd really done was hang a few pictures and arrange the furniture.

Madelyn moved into the bedroom, and couldn't stop herself from double-checking the closet. She peeked under the bed, too. No monsters.

Even so, she waited for Hudson to come inside before she started toward the shower. He mumbled something that she couldn't quite hear and then she turned on the water. Slipping out of her clothes made all the difference in the world. Standing in the shower as warmth sluiced through her caused her to release the breath she'd been holding. It had felt like she'd been holding that breath ever since the call had come from Ed Staples.

The realization of just how much her life was about to change was staggering. And to prove it, she could hear her ringtone in the other room pumping out almost constantly. She thought about Harlan and the promise she'd made to allow him to break the story.

Surely, he would understand. Or maybe he'd fire her. Suddenly, work was the last thing she could concentrate on. A warm shower and her own bed would go a long way toward making life straighten itself out again.

None of which mattered without Hudson.

The bathroom door quickly opened and then closed. The room stilled. The only other sound was the lock.

The mirror wasn't completely fogged up, so she saw him clearly. Owen.

Cornered, Madelyn searched for anything to use as a weapon. She picked up a shampoo bottle and threw it at him but he batted it away. She screamed.

"Your boyfriend is outside with the cops. No one can hear you," Owen said, and there was a strangely calm quality to his voice that sent an icy shiver down her spine.

"We can talk about this, Owen. Settle this out of court." Madelyn kept her eyes on him as she reached for a towel. Thoughts of the self-defense class she'd taken when she was younger ran through her mind.

"You're lying." He took a threatening step toward her. She reacted by jabbing her fist toward his face in panic. And then she felt an iron grip around her forearm as she tried to pull back. He was bigger than her, obviously, and surprisingly strong. His wild eyes said he was long past talking at this point.

"I'm not. I promise," she countered.

"You just had to keep pushing. You wouldn't be happy until my reputation was ruined," he said, and there was so much anger in his voice, his eyes. "This was supposed to be simple. I'd kill you and problem solved. It was perfect. No one would've suspected me after learning that you were a Butler."

"Wait. How'd you know?" The admission stunned her.

"There are spy devices that can be placed on work desks and in homes," he said.

He'd believed her to be having an affair with her coworker. It all made sense now.

His other hand came up to her throat, and in the next moment, the back of her head slammed against the tile of her shower. He was in her face and her body revolted at his touch.

He ran his finger along her jawline and she tried to turn her head away from him but he forced it back. "Look at me, bitch. I want my face to be the last thing you see before you die."

That was all it took for a burst of adrenaline to strike. Madelyn shot her knee up to his groin. Owen's eyes bulged, his grip momentarily weakened but not enough for her to gain the upper hand. He pressed his body against hers, essentially closing off any space for her to be able to do that again, and she wanted to vomit.

Her hands flew everywhere, trying to gain purchase as the room started to spin. She gouged at his eyes and he released a string of curses.

He was too strong and she was losing consciousness. Madelyn couldn't scream. Reasoning would do no good.

But when Owen pressed his lips to hers, she bit and at the same time used all the strength she had for a final push. She bucked off the wall and he took a step backward, caught his legs on the tub and tripped.

Owen splayed out on his back and she jumped over him as she screamed with everything she had inside her. Her neck felt like it had rope burn where his hands had been and she had a hard time catching her breath as she gripped the doorknob, half expecting to be pulled back any second.

The door opened partially before the cold fingers closed around her right ankle. She tried to shake his hand off but he was too strong.

"Hudson! Help!" she shouted.

"I already said your new boyfriend can't hear you." Owen's other hand caught her other ankle. His hands felt like vise grips.

Madelyn grabbed on to the counter for leverage and tried to kick out of his grasp. Panic had her heart pounding her chest. Panic because she thought she might never see the cowboy again. She grabbed her brush from the counter and threw it at Owen's face. He turned his head in time and she missed. Her hairspray can was next.

With shaking hands, she pulled off the cap and then sprayed it toward his face.

That got him coughing and the distraction gave her a chance at freedom. She dashed down the hall and toward the front door. A chair had been secured under the knob.

By now there was pounding at the door as someone tried to break through from the other side.

"Hudson!"

"Madelyn, can you move whatever's blocking the door?" he asked, and his voice was the only thing calming her racing pulse.

"I'll try." The kitchen chair was secured pretty tightly. Adrenaline and fear had her panicking too much to think clearly. Could she jump out a window? As she glanced left, she saw Owen emerge from the hall. He had something in his hands and she knew for certain if she couldn't get this door open it was all over.

Madelyn pushed at the chair and rattled the door handle. She'd managed to unlock it but couldn't think clearly.

"Think you can escape me?" A shrill sound tore from Owen's lips. "I'll follow you. You know that white sedan? It's me. The man in the tree line? Me. The cops can't catch me before you get what you deserve."

"Everyone knows it's you. Go through with this and you'll spend the rest of your life in jail," she said.

"You wouldn't drop the charges, Madelyn. My reputation is already over." He dived at her knees, knocking her onto the unforgiving wood floor.

Madelyn screamed as her head made contact. She tried to scramble to her feet but Owen was on top of her, his fists banging against her head, her body. After taking a boot to the midsection, she curled into a ball to protect herself. Another hard kick landed on the back of her head.

Owen was spewing curse words as he beat her.

Madelyn curled into a tight coil, rolled onto her back and sprang toward him. Her feet connected with his knees. His legs buckled and he hit the floor next to her.

There'd been three loud thumps against the door. It exploded open on the fourth.

And then Hudson was there, on top of Owen, wrestling him to the ground. An officer was working beside him, restraining Owen's feet.

Owen got off a good kick and the officer

stumbled into Hudson. In the confusion, Owen managed to get free and grab the officer's gun. He came up standing, pointing the gun from the officer to Owen to Madelyn.

"Everybody back up," he shouted, and his expression was feral. "Put your hands where I can see 'em."

All three of them complied as he took a step toward Madelyn. "Wrap a blanket around yourself."

Madelyn pulled the cotton blend from the back of the couch and did as he said.

"Take it easy," Hudson said in a soothing voice, hands up. "We can work this out."

"There's no 'we.' Madelyn's coming with me. She knows what she did wrong." Owen looked at her. "Get over here."

She looked to Hudson, who nodded almost imperceptibly.

"I said, 'Now!'" Owen's gaze narrowed.

"Okay," Madelyn agreed, moving next to him.

He stepped behind her, wrapped an arm around her midsection and placed the officer's gun at her temple.

Madelyn gasped. The look on Hudson's face nearly brought her to her knees.

"It'll be okay," he reassured her, but he looked hollowed out.

All she could think was *How?* She didn't ask. Because it would never be all right again if Owen got her out that door and into his vehicle. Everyone seemed to realize it.

One last glance at the cowboy as she was being ushered out the door and he mouthed three words that renewed her strength and brought a sense of calm over her... *I love you.*

She loved him, too. She'd known it almost from the minute they met. Before that Madelyn had never believed in love at first sight. She believed in attraction. A pull. But never real love. And yet she knew this was special. Real.

If she didn't act fast, her life would be over.

She knew that if Owen got her to a second location there'd be no walking out. He'd have a secure place where he'd torture her to his heart's content before killing her.

The time for action was…

Now!

Madelyn signaled to Hudson with her eyes. And then she dropped to the floor, catching Owen completely off guard. His eyes had been focused behind him at the officer and Hudson.

Before he could react, Hudson dived on top of him and Madelyn clamped her arms around his legs. She heard a snap when Hudson made contact and figured one of Owen's legs had just broken.

He shrieked in pain as he was pinned to the ground outside of her apartment door. Hudson's knee staked his arm and Owen's hand flew open, releasing the gun. Madelyn scrambled to get it before Owen could recover. She gripped it as the officer rushed toward them. She scooted as far away from Hudson and Owen as she could as the two men fought.

Owen was no match for Hudson in a fair fight and the cowboy easily dispatched him. Before Owen could mutter another curse, he'd been flipped over onto his stomach; his face was eating concrete and his hands were being zip-cuffed behind his back.

The officer immediately retrieved his weapon and holstered it. He called it in and helped Madelyn to her feet.

Embarrassed, she secured the blanket around her.

"You can go inside," the officer said, taking pity on her. But she couldn't. She needed to see Owen being taken away in the squad car. It was the only way she'd ever feel safe again.

"Enjoy spending the rest of your life behind bars," Hudson said as he walked Owen to the back seat of his former boss's SUV and personally secured him inside the vehicle.

As soon as they drove off, he turned to Madelyn. There was so much emotion in his eyes as he took her in his arms.

"I thought I'd lost you," he said into her hair, and his voice rolled over her. "Let's get you inside."

Madelyn walked beside him. Her place was a wreck and it felt a lot like her insides. The nightmare was over. It would take a little time to come to terms with that, but Owen was going to jail. He couldn't hurt her or any other woman again.

She threw on yoga pants and a workout shirt and pulled her hair into a ponytail. "Being here is strange."

Hudson had been watching and there was so much appreciation in his eyes. There was another emotion, too, and she couldn't quite pinpoint it.

"I meant what I said before, Madelyn." He walked to her and took her in his arms. His strong heartbeat against her ear brought so much comfort. "I love you."

She looked up at him. Tears threatened. Not tears of sadness but tears of joy. "I love you, too, Hudson."

"I've been waiting for the right words to tell you that I don't want to live without you. I love you and I want you to come home with me to live. Permanently." He didn't wait for a response. Instead, he tilted her face up and kissed her. "But I understand if that's not what you want."

"I'm ready to build a new life with you," she said, and she felt him exhale against her chest. "You should know that I intend to keep working. Maybe not as a journalist but I need to keep writing even if it's a blog. And I intend to make amends with my new family, the Butlers. Can you still love me if I claim my birthright?"

"I don't care what you call yourself as long as we belong to each other," he said without hesitation. "Besides, I know who you really are. You're brave, intelligent, beautiful. And if you'll have me, I'll stick by your side for the rest of my life."

"Forever sounds like a great place to start" was all she said before he picked her up off her feet and held her. "And just to clarify, I'm saying yes."

He kissed her, long and slow. "Let's go home."

And she wanted to tell him that in his arms, she was already there.

* * * * *

LET'S TALK

Romance

For exclusive extracts, competitions
and special offers, find us online:

f facebook.com/millsandboon

⊙ @millsandboonuk

𝕏 @millsandboon

Or get in touch on 0844 844 1351*

For all the latest titles coming soon,
visit millsandboon.co.uk/nextmonth

*Calls cost 7p per minute plus your phone company's price per
minute access charge

OO 2982189 X DO